Rad...

CHRIST...

RED FOX

*For Mopsa, Kate, Peter, Alex, Matthew,*
*Hannah, Joanna and Henry*

A Red Fox Book

Published by Random House Children's Books
20 Vauxhall Bridge Road, London, SW1V 2SA

A division of Random House UK Ltd
London Melbourne Sydney Auckland
Johannesburg and agencies throughout the world

Copyright © Christine Purkis, 1997

1 3 5 7 9 10 8 6 4 2

First published in Great Britain by
The Bodley Head 1997

Red Fox edition 1999

The right of Christine Purkis to be identified as the author of this work
has been asserted by her in accordance with the
Copyright, Designs and Patents Act, 1988.

Printed and bound in Norway by
AiT Trondheim AS

Papers used by Random House UK Limited are natural, recyclable products
made from wood grown in sustainable forests. The manufacturing processes
conform to the environmental regulations of the country of origin.

RANDOM HOUSE UK Limited Reg. No. 954009

ISBN 0 09 921012 6

# 1

*Behind the waterfall where the Waterfolk dream their dreams, Anno, the Keeper of the Circle, stirs. Sensing the paling dawn light, he uncurls his limbs and stretches awake. The spangles on his tail catch the light filtering through the curtain of water. Anno reaches out to the stone shelf above his head and takes his grey shale comb. First he must coax any tangles from his long hair until it gleams with a soft radiance.*

*It is time to prepare the chamber for the day.*

*As the new sun rises, so the other Waterfolk will come from their dreaming and congregate in the chamber for their grooming and their circle time. It must be made ready for their coming and this is Anno's task.*

*The pebbles must be arranged in a small circle on the rock floor. They glow as white as chalk and sparkle with delicate seams of crystal. Collected from the river-bed by the Waterfolk and their ancestors, they now sit magically defining the truth, the space which is within, the O.*

*It is Anno who, in each new morning's light, must fill the stone bowl with fresh water from the waterfall. He must sprinkle this water with his shaker of river-*

1

*weed over the face of the circle he has made until it glistens darkly.*

*He moves back, draws a long sweet breath, and allows the film of skin to close over his eye.*

*All is prepared.*

'Indian summer. They said so on the news,' Jo declared, licking the dripping edges of her ice-cream, trying to stop it from ruining her white T-shirt. Her fine brown hair was pulled back from her face and secured in a stubby pony tail by a fluorescent-pink scrunchie band. Tendrils of loose hair wisped round her cheeks and caught in the ice-cream. Jo sucked them, then pushed them back behind her ears with irritation.

'This is brilliant!' She waved her arms at the blue sky, the sun, the ice-cream, her bare legs, her roller-blades. A pair of mirrored sunglasses dangled from a rainbow string round her neck. She could see better without them anyway, her wide hazel eyes absorbing the light, not puckered and squinting like her friend Tash's.

'Usually pouring down in September.' Fizz skidded his skateboard to a halt, jumped on the back end and caught it as it leapt to his hand like a well-trained dog. As ever, he wore a baseball cap with green and blue stripes and the logo of a team he'd never heard of. It was round the wrong way so the long peak shaded his neck and a small tuft of brown hair stuck out of the arch above the plastic strap across his forehead.

The children were standing under a thirsty-looking horse chestnut tree, its large hands already yellow and curling. The tree was near the estate where they all lived, and the road beneath was littered with sticks and broken branches and the occasional empty conker case.

'I told you there weren't any conkers – we looked last week,' Tash told Fizz, not that she minded stopping for a moment. It gave her a chance to save the last melting fragments of her ice lolly. Tash had pale and blotchy skin. She hated the heat, which brought her out in a rash and made her irritable and snappy. A white visor shaded her eyes, but her hair stuck up above it, orange curls refusing to be tamed. Her cycling shorts were Lycra and lime green. She should have worn a long-sleeved top, but today she had risked a T-shirt with 'I love Pandas' splashed over it.

'There's one right up there,' Fizz pointed out.

'You'll never reach it,' Tash told him without looking up, but Jo was already selecting missiles from the litter of broken branches at her feet.

'It's always boiling hot soon as school starts,' Tash continued, lobbing her lolly stick over the wall into the park.

'Fifty-pound fine!' Jo called out. 'I saw! That's rubbish you're chucking about.'

'Come off it! Bio-degradable, wood. Anyway, you're throwing wood around – same difference. And you're just being vandals,' Tash replied.

'That conker's going to come down anyway, isn't it?' Jo pointed out.

'We're just helping!' put in Fizz, grinning.

'Oh yeah? Just smashing up all the branches – great help! How would you like it?'

There was no answer to that but it didn't stop Fizz and Jo.

'Yeah! Got it!' Jo shouted.

'Bull's eye!' shouted Fizz at exactly the same time.

They were so busy arguing about whose stick had struck the winning blow, it was actually Tash who squeezed through the broken railings, shaped like spears, to pick up the fallen trophy. Before the others realised what was happening, she was waving it in triumph in front of their noses.

'Finders keepers!' she taunted them.

'Give us it!' said Fizz.

'No way, José!'

But Fizz would fight – even Tash, his best friend, and even for a measly conker – and Tash knew it.

'I've got loads at home.' She handed it over. 'Anyway, come on, you lot – I've got to get back. My mum'll kill me!'

It was a possibility; unlikely, but she'd come reasonably close in the past. Tash could be a 'right royal pain' as Jo's mum put it, and even Tash had to agree this was fair. It was not worth getting into a fight this evening, of all evenings. Tash was off the next day to live with her dad

and his new girlfriend on a farm in Wales somewhere. Well, Tash had *said* it was a farm but Jo's
mum had looked doubtful when Jo told her.
Her mum remembered Shaun, Tash's father,
before he moved away – laid back to the point
of falling over.

A central point between their three houses,
the chestnut tree was the place where the kids
usually met. They often lingered there, hoping
to find excuses to stay 'hanging out' together,
but there were usually more pressing reasons to
split them up. Today, Tash had to get back to her
mother, and though Fizz never had to get anywhere, Jo rarely stayed long without Tash. And
there were always her mother and brother at
home.

Jo left her roller-blades at the side of the house
and went in through the back door.

'You're late,' her mother remarked.

'Saying goodbye to Tash,' Jo reminded her
lightly.

'Oh sorry. Poor Jo!' She gave her daughter a
concerned look and would have given her a big
hug too, but the shovelling of food into the
Blob's open mouth could not be interrupted.

The Blob had been called the Blob ever since
he had been just that, a blob, when Jo had first
seen him on the scan in the hospital. Not such
a little blob now, oh no! His legs were so fat his
knees had disappeared and he was so heavy to

carry around that Jo's mum had developed backache, requiring expensive visits to the osteopath.

Most evenings now, since Jo's mum had strained her back, they bathed the Blob together. Jo lifted him out, wrapped him in his alphabet towel and handed him, like a parcel, to her mother.

Jo's mum sat on the lavatory and patted him dry while Jo trawled the bath for ducks, yoghurt pots, boats and the odd flannel.

'You hungry, Jo?' she asked, forcing the Blob's legs into a pair of blue and red pyjamas.

Jo nodded.

'I'll get some tea soon – or shall we have fish and chips?'

Jo shrugged.

'My purse is on the side.'

'Why should *I* get it?'

Normally her mother would have said, 'Why should *I*?', but as she didn't, Jo was hardly surprised when, halfway through her battered cod, eaten on their laps in front of the television, her mother said, 'I'm just going next door for a bit, Jo – I won't be long.'

'Why?'

'For a natter – come and get me if Blob wakes up.'

Jo slumped back in the chair, staring grumpily at the screen.

'Don't make a fuss, Jo – having a chat with

my friends is the only way I can be such an understanding, level-headed, easy-going parent to you!'

'Huh!'

'Bye!' Her mum blew a kiss, then stopped in front of the mirror in the hall to pull a comb through her black curly hair.

Jo's mum always said not to answer the phone if she wasn't there, but how could Jo be expected to let it ring and ring like that? Anyway, it might be burglars finding out if there was anyone at home or the call might even be for Jo herself. It was.

'You took your time.'

'Tash!'

'Where were you?'

'On the loo.'

They both giggled.

'Dad's not coming till the evening. Let's go somewhere.'

'Tomorrow?'

'Yeah.'

'What about school?'

'What about it?'

'Tomorrow's your last day!'

'Wrong – today was my last day! Be at the tree at eight-thirty. We can go to the brook.'

'Bikes, then.'

'Bikes – and tell Fizz.'

'Why are you whispering?'

'Why do you think?'

'Oh, OK.'
'Got to go. Be there!'

# 2

*The Waterfolk are dreaming in their smooth caverns behind the waterfall. They feel the light around them glowing and pink. At this time of day, it is the habit of the Waterelders to meet together in the larger chamber to comb each other's hair.*

*They sit round the pebble circle which Anno has formed, their silver-scaled limbs tucked to the outside, while each attends to the tresses of the one in front: pale, silvery-pink, waist-length. Their hair, though slow-growing, is never cut from the day they are born bald except for a suspicion of finest down. And in this circle, smoothing hair till it shines pink in the morning light, they chatter in their silent way, for they have no ears, no mouths. They send out thoughts on invisible waves: images, words, ideas, which travel instantly from one to all. A thought forms in one mind and immediately it is received in the minds of all the others, received and responded to, perhaps, or received and dwelt upon.*

*Twice a day they form their circle, in the morning light and as the sun sets. And it is in this evening time that they tell their stories, Dreams of the Past, told by the elders to the youngers so they may keep them in their hearts and their memories as treasure.*

9

The morning time, for the Waterurchins with their spiky hair, is one of play. Eager to be active, they slip sideways through the curtain of water and out into the strange and thrilling light which momentarily dries the skin until it tightens. The first game is to see who dares stay out in the air before diving deep into the cooler waters, turning, swirling, twirling in the eddies and currents, catching hold of the weeds and coiling themselves around thicker stems, then hiding there, invisible, before ambushing an unsuspecting friend. Or tickling the ducks' feet, mimicking the bobbing of the coots and moorhens, racing the fishes, teasing the transparent water prawns, tweaking the tails of the tadpoles in spring, leap-frogging the frogs in summer.

It is only the Paddlefeet they are shy of. Infrequent visitors to the river in the cold and dark parts of the turning circle, the Paddlefeet arrive with the sun and the light. When they stay on the banks, casting only their shadows on the water, they are harmless enough. But their invisible lines of thread are hazardous, and their bright, bobbing floats and feathers conceal deadly hooks. The fish fall for them every time. The Waterfolk have felt their desperate flapping and flailing when caught and learned to be wary.

Paddlefeet are what they most fear, Paddlefeet who arrive when the water runs warm and the Waterfolk are at their most sluggish. They invade suddenly and without warning, churning the water with their vast, thrashing limbs and giant paddle feet. Perhaps they mean no harm, but they boil the water to a treacherous confusion. They even clamber over the rocks with those clumsy paddle feet, probing the crevices with their giant toes.

The fishes leave the area, any sensible frog stays close to the river-bank and the coots hide in the reeds. The Waterfolk gather their Wateryoungers into the deepest recesses of the rock until the pink light has drained from the sky. There is no danger from Paddlefeet in darkness.

Today is a day of warmth and light. It is a special day: a Day of Naming. It is time for the youngest Waterfolk to leave their cradle and be given an identity.

Their dreaming, their feeding, their growing has made the cradle of their first dreams too small now. Their tails are curled round at the lip of the rock while their heads touch the stone which curves over them. The first sheen of hair, fine and silver, dusts their heads. They have watched the other Wateryoungers slip through the curtain. They have caught their laughter and delight. They are ready to play.

Nonno, the Giver of Names, takes the bowl which Anno hands to him. The bowl is a perfect circle. It holds their truths; it also holds the water, without which the Waterfolk will perish.

The Waterfolk lay down their combs. Each Guardian of a Wateryounger thinks of the little form curled in its dreamspace and calls it forward to the circle. The Waterurchins who already have their names are summoned from their play. They slip through the water curtain, zinging electric blue with energy and life, and form an outer circle behind the elders, some of whom now cradle a Wateryounger in their laps.

Nonno moves round the circle, stopping each time he reaches a younger. He stops, his mind has no thought. And there, suddenly, is the name, and each name has the O within it.

'Mox!' he pronounces. 'Zoy! Lol!'

And as the name is given, the urchins call it out and the named one can slip away to join them in their games.

Two of the tallest urchins, Axos and Odol, take the hands of the smallest, Mox and Lol and Zoy. 'Hold tight!' they command.

The bigger urchins sit on the lip of rock while small arms are latched round their necks. Thus secure, the Wateryoungers break suddenly into the world they have never known. It is brilliant, it is fire, it pinches the skin and blinds the mind, as immediately they are plunged down into green depths. They feel the pull of water against their bodies as they move, but their hands are clasped tightly around the necks of their guides and there is no fear. It is exhilarating, the movement: the diving, the turning, the twisting, slicing through the cool depths, rising in a fizz of bubbles to break the surface before folding back over and diving again. And all the time there are delicious sensations against the skin: a strange tingling of different temperatures, a thicker feel near the mud of the river-bottom, a clear flow near the frothing surface; the occasional brush with a tickly frond of weed, the flick of a fish's tail, the slap of a duck's foot.

*Next time, they will not wait for the others to come for them, to take them on their backs. They will slip down the rock face alone. Tentatively at first, but the speed of their inevitable fall will be enough to accelerate them into diving and rising, twisting and turning fearlessly, independently.*

*For now, still clamped to the backs of Axos and Odol, they learn to play: chasing, spinning, racing, teasing. And how they all scream and whoop and shriek inside themselves with laughter! Each head is filled with wild sound. But the old fisherman sitting on the bank, who comes here for peace and quiet, hears only the watery gurgles of the river, the occasional plip or plop of a fish breaking the surface, and perhaps the clear evening song of a lone blackbird.*

The fisherman, having abandoned his spot on the river-bank, stood at the bar in The Rod and Perch supping a pint.

'Beautiful day, Tom,' said the barman.

'So say, Jack, so say,' the fisherman answered gloomily.

Jack, polishing the glasses, hesitated. 'Any luck?'

'Nah! Summat's up, Jack, and I don't like it. Water's down again – no rain, see – and there's not enough for the poor old fish. That's how I sees it, anyroads.'

'Well, I'm not complaining – good for my line, Tom.' Jack surveyed the customers sitting outside and congratulated himself again on investing in those umbrellas and plastic tables.

Tom stared into his glass. A fisherman, man and boy, on this stretch of the river for over eighty years, and he'd never seen anything like it. There was a feeling of melancholy inside himself and no accounting for it.

'Ah well, best be getting home . . .'

Nothing else to be done, though he hated the feeling of returning with nothing to show for a morning's work. Not even stories of the ones that got away or the ones he'd thrown back. Still, no one to tell the tales to now either – except Toby, and he'd not understand. Wouldn't care if he *could* understand. Toby's feeling about fish in his bowl was clear: not fit food to offer a dog. That look in his eyes!

Tom chuckled out loud as he strolled back along the river-bank, rod and reel in their weathered leather cases in one hand, stool and empty canvas bag in the other. Over the hump-backed bridge he went, pausing briefly to look down at the waterfall and the pool beneath him. There, lurking in the shadow cast by the bridge, was a brown trout, unmoving, pretending to be a shadow himself.

'Well, wouldn't you know!' The sight of this plump fish restored Tom's spirits a little. Perhaps, after all, he had been overreacting, making a mountain out of a molehill. Perhaps the rains would come.

He was just turning away back home when,

from the corner of his eye, he caught sight of something. A movement. Near the trout. Something blue, wasn't it? A drop of blue, essence of all blues, in the murky grey water, moving like a ripple against the current. Tom caught his breath. He wanted it to be so much! All these years he'd been hoping for another sighting, a confirmation. But when he looked again the spark was gone, as always, leaving him doubting. Probably an insect, the wind ruffling the water's surface, a chance catching of the light. Yet Tom failed to convince himself because, inside, he carried that memory of a blue liquid jewel. He knew what he knew, even if it didn't make sense. He'd carried the secret, boy and man, and never wondered what to do with it. Until now. Now, when his river was changing and danger was in the air, it might be time to pass the secret on.

*Behind the waterfall, while the youngers play outside in the river, a sobering thought cuts through the Waterfolk's idle gossiping.*

*'There is still no rain!'*

*Some continue their combing, quietly and seriously, but the thought is bleached in their minds.*

*'The water level is falling!'*

*It is not the first time this thought has been there. It is true. They all know it. True – and they are helpless.*

*The Waterurchins, carrying the exhausted and excited Wateryoungers, slip back sideways through the waterfall, just as the evening light is burnishing their world. The elders quickly blank out the thought, mindful that their young ones shall not catch their anxiety. Quickly, but not quickly enough.*

*Axos, the first to climb back into the chamber, catches the thought before it fades. He catches the fear and it runs through his body from the tips of his spiky hair to the ends of his spangled limbs like a shiver.*

# 3

Getting in touch with Fizz was always difficult, for he wasn't on the phone. If it had been up to Jo, she'd not have bothered. She and Tash could have a good time without him. But it *was* Tash's last day and Jo *had* promised . . .

She left the house ten minutes earlier than usual that morning.

'Where are you off to?' asked her mum suspiciously. 'You're not late yet!'

Jo mumbled something about netball practice and before her mother could do more than repeat, 'Netball practice?' she was off, wheeling her bike down the garden path and stuffing her mouth with a last slice of toast and marmalade.

Fizz's front gate lay on its side, long grass and dandelions pushing their way between the rotting wooden slats. Several old cars blocked the entrance to the house. Two had their wheels off and doors hanging open; only one had a bonnet which was closed. No sign of life. No curtains drawn either. But then maybe no curtains to draw.

'Tash – I'm doing this for you!' Jo said, feeling noble. She propped her bike against the hedge and began to tiptoe up the path to the front door. She'd never have done it, not even for Tash, had she known what was in the old Robin Reliant to the right of the path. She had taken only a few steps when the car rocked on its brick base alarmingly, and a huge, slavering, brindled dog hurled itself towards her. Jo shrieked and froze to the spot. Mercifully, the dog was inside the car but she saw him crash into the window, obviously leaping for her throat. Infuriated by his captivity, he threw himself again and again at the window, snarling, yelping, whining all at the same time.

The moment Jo screamed, Fizz's head appeared at the bedroom window. His hair was sticking up like a brush, but he appeared at the door a couple of seconds later, cap on head, fully dressed, and slammed the door behind him.

'Don't worry about him.' He jerked his thumb in the direction of the Robin Reliant. 'Hasn't ever escaped – yet!' he added cheerfully. 'Where we going?'

'The brook. Tash's last request.' Jo thought she'd say that with a kind of smile. Joke! But instead she ended with the embarrassing feeling that she was going to burst into tears. Checking anxiously to see that Fizz hadn't noticed, Jo swallowed down the furball stuck in her throat. 'She told me to tell you.'

Fizz nodded, then bent down and pulled his

bike from under a green tarpaulin near a heap of spare car parts.

'Let's go!' he whooped as he raced off down the road.

Fizz was first to arrive, closely followed by Jo. They threw their bikes into the long wheat-coloured grass and flopped flat on the river-bank, panting for air like two stranded fish.

'I won – gold!' Fizz announced, punching the air in victory.

'I wasn't racing,' said Jo, pulling the scrunchie band from her hair and pushing her fringe back away from her forehead, where it was stuck down with sweat.

'OK. Let's go!' Fizz sprang to his feet, ripping off his shirt, stepping out of his trainers by treading on the backs and kicking them into the air as he ran.

'Hey, hang about! That's not fair!' Jo was searching for her towel and swimming costume. When she'd found them, she then had to wrap the towel round herself and wriggle and struggle and pull.

Fizz was already in the water, splashing and blowing like a baby whale.

'Don't dive!' he shouted as Jo lifted her arms over her head.

'Why not?' she asked, being inclined to do exactly as he had told her not to.

'Too shallow.'

She jumped instead, and even though she

curled her knees up to her chin, her feet still touched the soft mud at the river-bottom. The water round them was churned and brown.

'Brilliant!' Jo shouted, secretly glad she had heeded his warning.

Fizz dived and surfaced just beside where she was swimming. He grabbed her legs and started tickling her feet.

'Don't!' screamed Jo. 'Let go. Help, I'm drowning!' She beat at the water with her hands and threw her head backwards, straining to keep her nose above the surface. Fizz was still pulling her down. She kicked out savagely.

'I mean it!' she gurgled at him. Couldn't he see that? He caught hold of her flailing leg and pulled her under again and she felt the weight of his hand on her head, forcing her down. It was panic she felt, blind panic for a second, before he released her and she rose to the surface spluttering and coughing and gasping for air.

'You jerk!' she shouted at him.

But Fizz didn't care – or else he didn't realise. She never knew which.

'Thanks a bunch!' Tash had arrived, breathless, on the river-bank.

'Where you been?' called Fizz cheerfully.

'Thanks for your help and concern I *don't* think,' she said. 'Gear got stuck, didn't it?'

'Did you fix it?' Jo called, back-paddling with her hands to keep afloat.

'No thanks to you!'

It didn't take long, it never did. Only a few

minutes later, all three were screaming and laughing and dive-bombing each other from the bank. Finally, hunger overtook them and they crawled out on to the grass to search their bags for food and drink.

'Now what?' Tash asked. The picnic was finished and it was only eleven-thirty.

'If it was spring we could get taddies,' said Fizz.

'We haven't got anything to put them in.'

'We could get frogs.'

'I know!' Jo sat up, excited by her own idea. 'We could build a raft!'

Fizz groaned.

'No – hold on, let me finish – and we could go over the waterfall!'

They chewed over the idea with dried grass stalks.

'OK. Let's do it!' Fizz said, suddenly leaping up.

'What with?' Tash asked, without moving.

'Come on – just look around,' Jo told her.

They were hunting for wood when Fizz came across Tom's tin of bait, forgotten in the fisherman's depression the previous evening. Fizz prized the lid off, unsuspecting.

'Urgh!' He recoiled in shock, but then took another look and was soon studying the seething white mass with fascination. 'Hey, Jo, look what I found!'

Jo was struggling with a dead tree trunk, trying to wrest it from the ground. 'What?'

21

'Come see!'

Waiting until the tin was right under her nose, Fizz suddenly pulled the top away and laughed like a madman. Jo jumped away, horrified, while Fizz threw back his head and roared. To his surprise, Jo sprang on him like a fury, pulling his hair, biting, trying to knock the tin out of his hand.

'Ow! Give over, only a joke. Give over, or I'll have to flatten you!'

He would have done, as Jo knew, but Tash, working nearby to smash up a wooden crate she had found under the willows, heard their fighting and intervened.

'Break it up.' She wrenched them apart and Jo fled in tears.

'What's going on?' Tash demanded.

'Oh, nothing,' Fizz said, then showed her the maggots.

'You jerk!' Tash told him.

'I hate you!' Jo shouted the words really loudly inside her head. But she wasn't going to let Fizz spoil everything, no way. Anyway, they *were* only maggots. It was just the shock, really.

She dried her eyes and wiped her nose on the back of her hand. As she did so, she saw some twine caught in the overhanging willow branches. It looked as though it had been caught there long ago when the river was last in spate; grey and sunbleached by now, and tangled with grasses and twigs, but twine nevertheless. By stretching herself full length along the branch she could just reach it, and although the branch sagged under her weight, she felt secure.

While Jo was absorbed in her unpicking she caught an unusual movement in the water beneath her: something small, something deep blue, something which flashed upstream against the flow of the water. It was caught in a moment of total clarity: the tiny head, the arms, the sequinned tail. Yet it vanished on the instant, as though the blinking of her eyes had wiped it away. Though the image was still printed clearly on her mind, she began to wonder whether she could have seen what she thought she had.

'What was that?' She blinked and screwed up her eyes, crunching the dark until it broke into stars, and then opened them wide to let in the bright light. She must be going crazy! With a shake of her head, she pulled the twine free and wound it into a little ball. Where was Tash? She could tell her. But there she was, working away with Fizz to free a piece of driftwood caught in the river weeds. She couldn't tell Fizz, no way. Not to have him sneer and call her barmy.

Without saying anything, she presented them with the twine and together they bound the logs and wood together, finishing them off with Fizz's laces. Carefully, they manoeuvred the fragile craft into the river, into the pool above the waterfall.

'Who's having first go?' Jo asked.

'I'll go second,' said Tash, secretly hoping the craft might have broken up by then.

'Jo?' Fizz offered. She knew he would want her to say no.

'OK.'

It wasn't such a big waterfall, only a drop of about two feet, and the water was neither particularly deep nor fast-flowing, but to Jo it might as well have been Niagara. She lay on her tummy, her legs dangling over one end, the other end up to her chin, and gripped the raft tightly with both hands. The other two waded out, pushing her into the river flow, then with a one, two, three, they gave a final push forward and she was on her own.

At first she hardly moved; then suddenly, there was no time for thinking, no possibility of control. It was happening! Left – crash – right – a push off with her right hand and foot – a crash on the left to her shoulder – then a froth of power and speed and bubbles as she hurtled forward and down, side to side and finally head over heels. At some point the raft was ripped from under her, leaving her spluttering but safe in the calmer water below the fall.

'You all right?' Tash asked as she pulled Jo up the bank.

'Yeah.' She nodded quickly, snorting water first down one nostril, then the other.

'Looked dangerous.'

She recalled that Tash had chosen to go second. 'Nah, piece of cake!'

'I'm not going head-first anyway,' Tash resolved.

She sat astride an even more unsteady craft, trailing her legs either side as stabilisers.

'You'll have to tuck your feet in,' Jo told her authoritatively.

Tash meant to but that sudden rush of water was so fast that she was taken completely unawares. She only had time to scream once before her foot crashed hard against the first big boulder on the right. Her mind had just registered pain when she was tipped sideways, hitting her arm on the second rock.

She rose to the surface red-faced, screaming and crying and snorting and half-laughing with the thrill of having done it, all at the same time.

'I killed myself!' she screeched.

Jo and Fizz hauled her out of the water to examine the damage. Blood was oozing from the gash on her arm. Fizz stood uncertainly as Jo dabbed at Tash's arm with one of his socks, donated for the purpose.

'That doesn't hurt so much – it's my ankle. It's killing me!' Tash said. She tried to stand, putting her arm round Jo's shoulders, but couldn't put weight on her right side at all.

'Get on that raft if you're going, Fizz!' Jo said impatiently. 'We can't wait all day.'

There was no one to push him off and no one to run along the bank shrieking and screeching, and although his descent was observed, there was no one in the pool at the bottom to see him arrive on a tidal wave of water fountaining around him in a spectacular display.

Or so he thought. He did not know about the single eye which peeped out from behind the flimsy cover of the water reeds and saw the boiling confusion of water and the thrashing limbs of a Paddlefoot.

'Did you see?' Fizz had to ask after he had picked himself up from the pool below the waterfall, knowing nobody had. 'Hey, look at your foot!'

'I know – it's swollen up. Can't even get my bloomin' shoe on,' Tash said, 'let alone cycle.'

'What are you going to do?' Fizz asked.

'She'll just have to sit on her saddle and we'll walk home,' Jo said.

'That'll take hours!'

'So, it'll take hours. Got a better suggestion?'

'Yeah, she can sit on my saddle and I'll ride her home. Two to a bike, like we used to!'

'What about *my* bike?' Tash asked.

'We'll hide it, or take it to the nearest house or something,' said Jo quickly.

The fisherman's cottage was the first house they passed. Tom, picking Bramleys from the old tree in his front garden, saw the two children on the one bike pedalling down the road and shook his head. He was right up in the fork of the tree, so neither Jo, wheeling Tash's bike, nor the other two parked at the gate, saw him. When he coughed and called out, Jo screamed and nearly dropped the bike.

'What can I do for you?' Tom called out.

'Please can we leave a bike here because my

friend has hurt her ankle and she can't ride it home? We'll collect it soon.'

'What have you been up to, then?' the old man asked, lowering himself from the tree. Tash hobbled forward, leaving Fizz at the gate. There was a small twig caught in the old man's silvery hair. Jo tried to avoid Tash's eye.

'Hit it on a rock,' Tash explained. Tom winced in sympathy.

'There's not as much water this year,' Jo said.

Tom looked at her strangely. 'I know it!'

'So, can we leave it? The bike?' Jo asked.

'What? Oh yes, that's fine by me. Put it in the shed.'

Jo wheeled the bike in and left it propped up against a stack of empty cardboard boxes.

'We'll come back for it soon,' she promised. 'We'd better get off now – thanks a lot.'

'Cheerio!' said Tom.

'Cheerio!' echoed Tash naughtily in a strong country accent and burst into giggles – until she stood on the damaged foot, forgetting for a moment then remembering suddenly and painfully. 'Oww!'

'Get on, then,' said Fizz impatiently. His breathing had only just calmed down after the short ride from the river to the old man's cottage and he was aware of the distance he had to go.

'Bye,' Jo called out. Tom was standing with one large Bramley apple in his hand. He still had the twig in his hair. 'And thanks!'

'Cheerio,' Tash called out again but Fizz was

silent and grim-faced as he strained to pull away up the lane.

Tom stood gazing down the lane long after the children had disappeared from his misty vision. He was still holding the apple in the palm of his hand as solemnly as if it had been an orb. Eventually he turned and walked back to his cottage. Toby, hearing his master's familiar tread, wagged his tail a couple of times in greeting but otherwise didn't stir. Tom sat heavily in his armchair. He passed the apple to and fro between his hands as he had done years ago with his cricket ball.

'Well, what do you think, eh, old chap? Is it time to pass on the secret? What do you say?' He nudged Toby with the toe of his boot affectionately and then, remembering, stooped to loosen his laces.

'This time I've got this feeling in my bones, see. Don't know if it's the weather or what, but as my mother used to say: feelings in the bones are feelings you should take seriously. Now that's something I'll bet you'd agree with, eh, old fellow?'

Toby stretched out his old legs and rolled a long low groan around in his throat.

'Couldn't have put it better myself,' said Tom.

# 4

*It is not until darkness falls that the Waterfolk dare to venture out from the deepest crevices in the rock. The first explosion of water as those huge Paddlefeet leapt into the pool from nowhere had shocked them into hiding. They had felt the raging of the water, seen the enormous lumbering forms and had shrunk back into the darkest cracks in their rock chambers.*

*Even so, they had been aware of the monstrous shapes crashing over their rocks, thundering down over their curtain of water. They had felt the thudding and vibrations on the stone and sensed the trails of iron-red warmth in the water, and recoiled. Their world had been shaken. They were left quaking.*

*Only one – Axos, the quickest Waterurchin – whose unique curiosity seemed to vanquish his fear, had actually ventured beyond the curtain of safety. Not for long, but long enough to feel the size of the Paddlefeet's presence, which was awesome, and to feel also their playful intention. Of that, he had not been afraid; that he had recognised.*

*He had slipped back unnoticed into the dreaming chamber and settled unobtrusively into a state where all his thoughts were suspended. It would not do for another young one to catch hold of them.*

*Now, as the sky flames and casts a golden light on the peaceful water, the Waterfolk relax out of their hiding places. Above the pool the gnats dance. In the now-peaceful water, the fish glide easily, occasionally flicking to the surface to dispatch a careless insect. A coot bobs along on the water reeds, and the frogs kick their way from lily pad to lily pad.*

*Tentatively, the Waterurchins slip through the falling water and, sensing the calm after the turmoil, slide into the water to play. Behind the waterfall, the older Waterfolk are grooming, sitting in their circle, silvered limbs curled over the blue stone. Again, their gentle talk is interrupted by that terrifying thought. It cannot be ignored.*

*'The water level is falling!'*

*They do not look forward, for now is all they know, but there is a feeling of darkness and something like dread which runs like a shadow round the circle. There is a silence, a blankness following this thought because it has displaced all others. They continue to groom but there is no thought of song or words of beauty such as are customary after the exchange of news – only silence.*

*When the pink light has nearly drained away, the Waterurchins and the youngers slip back through the waterfall curtain to join their elders. They bring with them an exuberance, an energy, a joy – and their bodies gleam with a clear blue light.*

*It is enough to dispel the gloom – and besides, their anxiety is not something the elders wish their youngers to catch. Each Waterurchin and Water-*

*younger curls itself comfortably into the lap of an elder, thus joining the circle. The limb-weary postures mark the start of the evening dream time. It is a time of pleasure for them all, old as well as young. Released from their anxieties, they can be drawn with safety into a clearer world where paths and outcomes are already known.*

*One of the Waterelders, a Dreamer of the Past, takes the water bowl from Anno and holds it in his hands. He stares at the surface of the water until he can see the reflection of his green eye staring back at him. In the centre of that reflection is the O, the dark O. This is where the dreams are to be found.*

*'Once, long ago, so it is told, there was a meeting, a crossing of our world and the world of the Paddlefeet, when one of the Paddlefeet helped us. It saved one of our youngers and returned him to us. This story must now be told!'*

*The other elders hang their heads and nod solemnly. The minds of the youngers are open, alert, because usually Dreams of the Past are full of warnings about the dangers of the Paddlefeet, their crashing limbs and selfish, clumsy ways.*

*'It was a day in early spring. The river was full and the waterfall thundering and the Waterfolk were safe in their chambers. It was the time when the salmon were jumping up and over us. All day long we could see their sinewy bodies twisting above us, flicking shadows of movement over our circle.*

*'We had warned the youngers not to go out, for when the river teems with young salmon, the water is a dangerous place for them to play. There was*

*one, however – Zoth was his name – who paid no heed to our warnings but slipped away through the curtain . . .'*

The young lad from the cottage had kicked his boots off and left them on the bridge. Barefoot was better, freer. His uncle had put the idea in his head by telling him that story about the bears and showing him pictures. If brown bears could catch salmon with those claws alone, surely he could catch them too with the net he had made from Mother's muslin, stained purple from last year's damsons. The river was high: in fact the sandbags were still in place by the cottage door, just in case. The meadows by the river were still underwater and the cows were complaining loudly in the farmer's shed.

Tom stood on the bridge next to his boots and watched. There was one! A salmon, there, and then gone – a flick of muscle, a right angle of fish in the air! And there was another, and another, leaping and straining, up and over. Marvellous! he thought. Amazing to struggle so against all that weight of water. Why couldn't they just settle for a different nursery downstream, somewhere beneath the waterfall?

From where he was standing, he could see the salmon trying to leap up the waterfall and failing time and time again. Yet, undeterred, they went on until they finally made it. Or didn't. Tom saw one fish lying on its side in the muddy shallows. He slithered down the bank and stood with his toes sunk into the mud. The fish stared at him with its one wide eye.

'I could have you for my tea,' Tom told it, 'but I don't know how long you've been dead, do I?'

And as he stretched forward to grasp it, holding on to the trunk of the willow tree with one hand, it flicked suddenly to life and swam out into midstream.

'Well, you had me fooled there!' Tom said and laughed. 'What a performer!'

At that moment a huge fish leapt out of the river just in front of him, showering him with a flick of its tail. He was just shaking the water drops from the front of his shirt when he saw something blue on his braces. It was oozy, almost slug-like at first glance, and he was about to flick it away when he heard a sound. Well, no, not really heard – not through his ears, anyway – more like felt the words in the very inside of his head.

*'No! Don't do that, please! Save me!'*

It was the little blue thing, had to be. And now, when Tom peered at it more closely, he could see it wasn't a slug at all, but some tiny organism, with minuscule pointed limbs and a face with one eye in the centre of it, a mere speck of green. The stripes of Tom's braces showed clearly through the pale body of this extraordinary creature.

'Heck! Whatever are you?' he asked.

'*I am Zoth. I was flicked through the air by the fish's tail.*'

The thoughts seemed to come first through the water and then through the air. Tom felt them first, and then he knew. He heard.

'*Put me in the water,*' the voice begged, '*but do not hurt me!*'

Tom wrung his hands together anxiously. A boy he might be, but his palms were as rough as tree bark.

'*No! You will pinch me and cause me pain.*'

'I didn't say anything,' Tom protested.

'*It does not matter if you do not speak the words. I hear them with my mind.*'

There were clumps of early water irises lining the edge of the water. The flowers were still tightly closed in white gauze but the young leaves were long and smooth.

'*Yes! I will climb on to the leaf and you will put the leaf in the water.*'

'*And that is what the Paddlefoot did, and Zoth was saved. He swam back to us and told his tale in the circle. And I tell it to you now,*' says the Dreamer of the Past, '*for you younger dreamers to keep and to treasure.*'

*It is a story which quickens Axos's heart and excites his mind. The story is told for them all but it speaks to him directly. He will keep it and, more than that, he will use it, picking from its words to form his own dream, a Dream of the Future.*

*What a supreme effort he must make to soften the*

*quick sharp thoughts, slow them down so they may
dissolve and allow his limbs to relax. He knows he
must feed and feed deeply, to store up nourishment
in his young body. He knows he may be called upon
and he will need all the strength he can muster.*

# 5

The very evening that Jo said goodbye to Tash she started missing her. As she was squeezing blue jellied toothpaste on to her brush, she remembered what she had seen, or thought she had seen, in the river, and wished she had told Tash. It preyed on her mind. When she pulled the covers over her head and closed her eyes, she could still see it, bright blue and swimming across the darkness. It was difficult to carry something like that and not talk about it, but she couldn't tell Fizz – no way. He'd just jeer at her. And her mum – well, she'd just warn her about sunstroke again.

The memory didn't fade, though. Over the next few days, she went to the library and looked up all manner of bugs and beetles in the reference books. She even searched through the CD Roms in the IT centre at school, but though the screen buzzed with a million iridescent, dancing, flying miracles, she never found anything which resembled that split-second sighting.

If ony she could write to Tash; at least then someone else would know. But how could she? She wouldn't know Tash's address until she wrote to her with it. Every day when the letter box opened and a shower of letters fell on to the mat, Jo rushed hopefully into the hall, and every day she was disappointed.

The solution came from an unexpected quarter.

It was around the beginning of October, when Jo's mum had already switched on the heating and Jo was wearing socks and sweaters again, that events started to change in Jo's household. It was time for the annual bleeding of the radiators, time to search for the radiator key and for Jo's mum, having sworn she could bleed them herself and wasn't going to waste good money on a plumber, to reach for the Yellow Pages, defeated. But not this year.

A man called Jim came round with his tool-bag one evening. Jo thought he was a plumber and chatted happily to him, even offering him mugs of tea as he worked. But when her mother appeared wearing a new blouse and earrings, smelling like a flower shop, and opened a bottle of wine, Jo started getting suspicious.

It turned out Jim was her mother's osteopath, not a plumber at all. He was such a handyman, though, that they soon had a new lock on the bathroom door, the electric kettle was mended and even the aerial on the television fixed, clearing the blizzards from the screen. Jo was almost won over.

Almost – but not quite. Her mother's

behaviour was embarrassing. She sang all the time and changed her T-shirt when the Blob was sick over it and, miraculously, her back seemed to be cured. The last straw for Jo was finding Jim shaving in the bathroom early one morning when she hadn't even been told what was going on. This, as she explained to her mother, was the final insult. She lived there too and she should have been consulted. To her surprise, her mother agreed with everything she said, kissed her and cooked her favourite chicken in garlic mayonnaise for supper. She even made Jo sandwiches for school lunch which she'd vowed never to do.

The best thing about Jim, as far as Jo was concerned, was that he had a van. One day, he made the mistake of parking it in the way of the garage door so that Jo couldn't get her bike in. He only did it the once.

Jo was quick to take advantage of his apology. 'You could run me out to the river to get Tash's bike,' she told him.

Her mother raised her eyebrows at her tone, but Jim said he'd be delighted.

Tash's bike was preying on Jo's mind. Every time she thought of Tash, which was at least once a day when the post came, she remembered her bike rusting away in the old man's shed.

They drove out to the stream together on the Saturday morning. Jo's mum had wanted to make it a family outing, but Jim was firm. He and Jo would go alone, it wouldn't take long. Jo caught sight of the meaningful look he shot her mother but ignored it. If he thought spending time alone with him would soften her up, he could think again.

They drove in silence mostly; Jo gazing out of the window, Jim tapping his fingers comfortably on the steering wheel. Just before they reached the brook Jo recognised the little cottage behind the hedge. 'Stop!' she yelled.

'Blimey, not much of a warning!' Jim said as he hit the brakes.

'It looks different,' Jo explained. 'The leaves have gone.'

They had – most of them, anyway – and the apples too, although there were still a few brown windfalls mouldering on the grass.

Tom, alerted by the squealing of brakes, appeared at his door. It was that little girl again. 'I wonder . . .' he said to himself as he scratched his chin.

'I've come for the bike,' Jo explained as she pushed open the gate. 'My friend's bike – you remember.'

'Come on your own, have you?'

At that moment Jim appeared, striding forward and stretching out his hand.

'This your dad?' Tom asked.

Jo shook her head furiously and flushed red.

'Just good friends!' Jim said quickly.

'Well,' Tom said, 'it's safe and sound as far as I know. Not that I've had much occasion to use it!'

The shed was a mess. Boxes of apples blocked the door and almost hid the bike, which was propped behind them against a row of old paint pots.

'I'll have it out in a jiffy,' said Jim cheerfully, rolling up his sleeves.

Tom and Jo stood together on the grass. He looked at her slowly as though scouring her face for a sign. How to begin . . .?

'So, not doing any more white-water rafting, then,' he started.

Jo shook her head and smiled.

'Not that you could, I don't reckon, not any more. The river level's dropped something shocking.'

'No rain,' Jo confirmed. 'They keep on about it on the news.'

'Ah well, it's true,' Tom said, looking at her again. 'So, you're quite a friend of the river, then?'

Jo nodded. 'We come here a lot!'

Tom took a deep breath. 'There's something a bit on my mind,' he began, 'and I've been looking for a person I could – ' But before he could explain any further, Jim emerged from the depths of the shed, wheeling Tash's bike.

'Hold on to it, Jo, while I put the boxes back,' he said.

The moment had passed. Tom shook his head and sighed. Not quick enough, that was his trouble! He'd give it one last try. 'Take a box of apples,' he told Jim. 'There's more than I'll ever eat my way through.'

And as Jim loaded the bike and the apples into the back of the van, Tom tried to reach Jo again, clumsily asking her questions. 'Where's your friend, then?'

'Tash? She's gone to Wales to live with her dad.'

'You'll be missing her,' he said.

'Yes,' Jo replied simply.

This was Tom's moment, but as he drew breath, Jim interrupted them again. 'Come on now! Your mum will be wondering where we've got to.'

Too late! He could only shake his head and call after her, 'Come again. Come soon! We'll do some fishing together next time. Do come!'

'All right,' Jo shouted back from the passenger seat.

'Nice old bloke,' Jim commented, pulling out and beeping his horn twice.

It was on the return journey that Jim found out Jo hadn't heard from Tash and didn't know where she was. 'Well, why not phone her mum?' he suggested. 'She'll know, won't she?'

It was such an easy solution, Jo was cross with herself for not having thought of it before. As soon as she got into the house, she went to the phone. It was as simple as that. She wrote that very night.

Dear Tash,

Why haven't you written? You'd better have a good excuse. I had to ring your mum for your address.

Ever since the day you left I've been wanting to tell you something. It's top secret but I know I can trust you. You know when we went rafting in the river and you hurt your foot? Well, when I was getting some string from the branches of this tree, I saw something in the river. I've never seen anything like it before. It was blue, bright blue, and the weird thing was, it had little arms and it sparkled.

Please don't say I'm mad, because I did see it, honest. I've been looking at books of insects ever since, but it wasn't an insect. I know it wasn't.

Please don't tell anyone. You are the only person who knows, apart from me. Write back at once.

Lots of love

Jo  XXX

PS We got your bike. Mum's new boyfriend has moved in. He's an osteopath. Thought she'd been having a lot of back trouble recently. He's got a van, so we went out to the old man's and got the bike. He gave us a box of apples, and he said he'd take me fishing if I go again.

And back came the reply:

Dear Jo,

Sorry I didn't write. You know how it is. Not doing anything and no time to do anything else.

It's weird, what you said about that creature. I don't know what it could be, but I'll keep my eyes peeled. There's a great waterfall near here and a river and everything. Plenty of rain in Wales, boyo. And plenty of sheep, too.

Dad doesn't fuss about what I do and don't do. Often I go out on the hills with him and the two dogs, Jones and Evans (Dad says it's a joke). They're Border collies – two girls, mum and daughter.

I've made a lot of friends – with sheep. All my neighbours are sheep. I look out of my window and what do I see? Sheep. When I go to sleep at night all I can hear are sheep. And guess what I don't count to get to sleep?

Well, got to go now. Cheerio!!

Lots of love

Tash XXX

PS May come down for Christmas – hope so.

PPS Don't worry about the bike. Too many hills here.

PPPS Haven't got a phone – but if you have an urgent message you could phone Weirdo on Llandovery 243. He's a friend of Dad's and he's got a male collie called Robocop which Dad is trying to get to mate with Evans. He's got three cats too and they're called Terminator I, Terminator 2 and Terminator 3.

# 6

November 14th was Jo's eleventh birthday. Her mum gave her a fishing rod. Jim fixed a special bracket on to her bike so she could clip on the rod which, though it came apart into two pieces, was nevertheless cumbersome to carry. She was all ready and on one cloudy though dry Saturday morning, she decided this was to be the day. After all, the old fisherman had promised.

Jo had assumed she would go by herself, but her mother had other ideas. 'You're not going alone, Jo! Ask Fizz to go with you.'

'Fizz? No, he's in all kind of trouble.'

'What kind?'

'Well, he found an old hub cap in his front garden and bowled it down the street.'

'That's not exactly a crime,' said Jo's mum.

'I know. But he bowled it into a policeman on duty who knows the family. He didn't think it was funny. He nicked him.'

'That's not fair – just because his brother is like that . . .'

'Brothers.'

'And his dad, I suppose. Well in that case, a

45

bit of fishing would do him good. You could help keep him on the straight and narrow, Jo.'

'Huh!'

'Don't be so negative – everything I suggest, there's something wrong with.'

'You said it.' Jo slouched in her chair, picking dirt out of the grains of wood in the table with a fork.

'Don't do that, Jo!'

'I'm just cleaning it.'

'I like it dirty. Why don't you do something? You're driving me mad!'

'I want to go fishing,' Jo repeated.

'We are not going round this again!' her mother shouted. 'Go down and ask Fizz. Go on, or I'll go and ask for you.'

Jo wheeled her bike slowly out into the road. She checked the chain, then thought perhaps she did need to put some more air into the tyres. After she'd pumped them up, there was nothing else to delay her. Reluctantly, she cycled off towards Fizz's house. Not going in again, no way, she comforted herself.

To Jo's relief, neither the dog nor the Robin Reliant were in evidence when she pulled up outside Fizz's house. Nevertheless she decided to stand at the gate and whistle. Fizz didn't have a doorbell so this was the traditional way of alerting him.

Immediately his head appeared at the bedroom window.

'You doing anything?' Jo called up, scuffing the gravel of the path with the toe of her trainer.

'Not a lot,' Fizz replied. 'Why?'

'Thinking of going fishing.' She paused. 'Wanna come?'

'Don't mind,' he shrugged.

'Don't have to!' Jo retorted.

Fizz shrugged again.

'Hang about,' he said. He emerged from the house, already astride his bike.

When they arrived at the old man's cottage, Jo propped her bike against the Bramley tree and knocked sharply on the green front door. Fizz lingered at the gate without dismounting. It took some time for Tom to come to the door, and when he did so, their unexpected arrival made him all of a dither.

'I'm Jo. Remember? I've brought my new rod. You promised to take me fishing.'

'Jo! 'Course I remember!' He rubbed his eyes as though to clear them. 'I did promise. I did.'

But again, she wasn't on her own. Looking up, Tom saw Fizz supporting himself on the gate, chewing gum.

'It's OK. That's Fizz. Remember? He's not as bad as he looks.'

Tom threw back his head and laughed. 'I like that,' he said. 'Not as bad as he looks! Come on in, young man.'

Tom led them into his kitchen. It was hot inside, suffocatingly so, the warmth coming from a huge black wood-burning stove which took up virtually a whole wall. In front of it, Toby sprawled, adding a pungent odour of old dog to the stifling air. As they entered, he lifted his head and wagged his tail a couple of times.

'Well, I'm going to have to disappoint you,' Tom said. 'We won't get much fishing today, I'm afraid. There's no fish left,' he added, shaking his head. 'Not on this stretch of the river, any roads. No rain, see – never seen the river so low in all my eighty-two years.'

Fizz, meanwhile, was trying to pick up logs with the fire tongs. He was snapping the claws together like teeth. He brought them up close behind Jo's ear.

'Fizz!' she hissed at him.

'We'll walk down to the river, eh?' suggested Tom. 'And have a look. I could do with a breath of fresh air.'

'Me too!' said Jo enthusiastically.

'And then I'll tell you what – we'll come back here, have a cup of tea. What say?'

'OK,' Jo agreed. Fizz nodded.

Tom unhooked a bright red checked jacket from the back of the kitchen door, pulled a woollen hat like a tea cosy over his ears, and out they went. Past the bikes abandoned by the Bramley tree, past the damson and the Victoria plum trees, their spiky branches standing out against the heavy sky, through the gate to the lane and then left to the river.

'Where's it gone?' cried Jo.

The waterfall, down which they'd rafted a few months before, had been reduced to a slow trickle, a quarter of its former strength and volume.

'The rain just never came,' Tom told her gloomily. 'Twenty years ago it were right up to here, see?' He pointed to a high tide mark on the bank, a distinct line separating the willows from their tangled roots, now crudely exposed in the bare mud.

'My cottage used to get flooded years ago – think of that! Sandbags at the doors and all sorts. Plenty of fish then, and kingfishers and dippers. We never see but the odd one nowadays. Even the old heron's a rare visitor now, and who can blame him. Go hungry, he would, if he were to stay around these parts. Look at that!'

He pointed to the muddy pool below the waterfall. 'Teeming, that used to be! Heaving! Plenty for the old heron, plenty for me, plenty for everyone.'

'Maybe it'll rain again soon,' said Jo, trying to find something cheerful to say. 'I mean, it's cloudy enough.'

'I know it, Plenty of clouds, no rain – don't feel right to me.'

'It's the greenhouse effect,' Jo told him auth-oritatively. 'We're doing it at school. Everything's getting hotter and drier. It's all these CFCs and gases – they're making a hole in the ozone layer.'

'Well, I don't know about that – holes and ozones and whatnot – but what I do know is, my river's dying in front of my very eyes and I'd never have believed it.'

Tom lingered on the bridge. He leant over the stone wall and looked into the water below. Nothing. Just the vague outline of his shadow thrown on to the dark surface of the water, his and the smaller shadows of the two children peering down to see what he was staring at.

'There's nought there to see,' he declared, shaking his head.

It was a sombre group that wandered back over the field this time, back to the stuffy cottage with its roaring fire and Toby lying by the hearth. After a strong cup of tea, Tom came up with a suggestion. 'Tell you what I'll do – I'll teach you two how to make floats for that smart new rod. How about it, eh? So's you won't have wasted your afternoon.'

Jo and Fizz exchanged glances, but the old man was obviously so keen, there was nothing they could do but agree. Tom brought an old shoe box from under the sink, full of chicken quills with the feathers shaved away, corks, paint and varnish pots. He showed the children how to singe the quill over a candle and fix on the cork, then the floats were ready for painting.

After all the talking, suddenly there was quiet, intense quiet as the three of them concentrated on the task in hand. The air was thick with the fumes of paint and varnish, overlaid on hot dog and a warm fishy smell. Tom, sitting at the head of the table, was the first to finish his work. He sat back idly, turning one of the older floats in his hand. He wasn't thinking, exactly, yet thoughts and images were swimming in and out of his mind: fishing images, river images.

He saw it again clearly, that instant flash of blue; it came and it went and he would never know for sure if it was what he thought it was. But then he saw the river disappearing in front of his tired old eyes, leaving the river-bed a cracked map of wrinkles and furrows, like the lines on his own face. He saw the waterfall dwindling to a trickle and then ceasing altogether, revealing the dried hollows in the rock which it had shielded for years, scoured and quite, quite empty.

He looked up sharply, suddenly alert. He had to say something now – while there was still time. Jo, unaware, was humming to herself as she put the finishing touches to her float. Yellow and blue like a macaw on the top, but dull and camouflaged on the rounded part as instructed. She imagined it bobbing in the water, held it up to see how it would appear to a fish. Suddenly a drop of blue flashed across her mind, liquid through liquid, almost like a bubble in a spirit level. She had seen it before, in the water. She looked up quickly. Tom was staring at her.

That was precisely the moment Fizz put down his brush and said, 'Yeah! What do you think of that?'

On the top, striped in reds and blues, he had written the words POW and ZAP, though the letters had smudged where the paint had run.

Tom shifted his gaze, took a deep breath and sighed. Relieved, that's what he felt. He hadn't been able to speak to the girl, but she knew. She knew, all right. He could tell by the way she looked at him.

'That's champion, lad,' he said gently.

Jo, released from Tom's glance, looked up at the window and realised with horror that the light was fading. 'We've got to go!' she announced, jumping up from the table. 'My lights aren't very strong, and I promised my mum I'd be back before dark. We'll come back soon, promise! Maybe do some fishing next time if it rains. Test out the floats.'

It wasn't quite enough. Tom fumbled in his pocket and brought out a crumpled brown envelope with '4 × 2″ brass screws' written on the back.

'Half a mo. Put your address on the front there for me, in case something happens – a fall of rain, a chance to fish – who knows . . . I could contact you then,' he said.

Jo had never seen a pencil worn right down to the stub like the one he handed her. She could hardly write with it, the way the wood dug into her palm. She wrote in block capitals so it was clear, knowing what old people's eyes were like.

'Good, good!' said Tom taking the envelope

from her and sticking it up on the mantelpiece next to the clock. He'd have to settle for that, an address and a promise.

'I hope it won't be too late!' he whispered to Jo.

'Too late? No, it'll be all right. It's just my mum gets all worried . . . you know . . .' She stooped to give Toby's head a quick fondle. 'Bye, Toby.'

Tom stood at the cottage door and watched them cycle away. Jo half-turned from the lane to wave and saw him still standing there, his arm raised in farewell, Toby behind him, just visible on the hearth rug in front of the glowing fire.

It was later and darker than Jo had realised. The road looked very white and the hedges tall and severe. Fizz was miles ahead, though she'd *told* him to wait for her. He never did what she wanted! If she was ever going to catch him she'd have to cycle Olympic fast. Jo stood up on her pedals and pounded after him.

Funny that, she thought as she hammered up the lane, sitting there dabbing blue paint on the float and that little blue thing swimming into her mind again . . . and looking up and the old man staring at her, reading her thoughts – or maybe she was reading his – and the river so low, as though the plug had been pulled out . . . and no one to talk to about it except herself.

'Oh, Tash, I wish you were here!'

Though her blood was beating in her temples and her legs were turning like pistons and her breath was rasping, it was the pain of missing Tash which made Jo feel she was about to burst.

'I want to talk to you!' she cried out into the cold night air.

*Behind the waterfall there is a gathering despair. Frosted dreams melt to dark foreboding. With the light shorter and the darkness longer, time feeds melancholy. Periods of bright crispness lift spirits momentarily. Scales shine briefly like cut diamonds. But these times are short and are followed by long stretches of darkness when anxieties rise to the surface of their dreaming.*

*Loddo, the Keeper of Time, sees the snow and the frost. He marks it and he knows that it is not enough. His mind is troubled. He has noted the way the water thirstily drinks the snowflakes landing on its surface, but he observes too how water can freeze into icicles. He hatches a desperate plan. Standing in the grooming chamber circle, he calls the others to him. They gather at his feet expectantly.*

*'All of us must participate. Every effort is needed. This year for our winter-fest each Being, old or young, will bring an icicle to me. We will store them here, on this shelf in the rock, store them against uncertainty.'*

*They do as they are bid, and soon the shelf, high and deep in the furthermost recesses of the chamber, is stacked high with daggers of ice, some thick and opaque, some thin as needles.*

*'Next,' says Loddo, 'each of us must gather snow crystals from the world outside. We will store them*

here in the stone channel which divides our grooming chamber from our dreaming places. We will make a river of snow against future uncertainty.'

And this is what the Waterfolk do, toiling instead of grooming, giving the labour of their hands against this threat which is unspeakable. But when Loddo stirs from his dreamings in the first flush of the new day, his hopes melt as the ice and snow have done. The high shelf is empty but for a dark streak which drips into the empty gully below. The white flakes of promise have dissolved into nothing in the quiet hours of darkness.

It is Axos who first wakes and catches Loddo's dark despair. As through Loddo's eye, he sees the emptiness and he feels the folly. The drops of melting ice on the bare rock are the tears of the Waterfolk. It is a sadness not to be borne. There has to be an answer and he, Axos, must find it.

'There must be a way!' His whole body flares bright blue with the force of the thought. 'There must be!'

'Yes – there has to be!'

Someone has caught his thought. He turns his head. It is Odol, his friend.

# 7

The week before Christmas it actually snowed. Only enough to lay the faintest dust of white over the school playground but still, the children, noses pressed against windowpanes, were in a frenzy of excitement. Plans were made: snowmen, snowball fights, tobogganing. But the snow only lasted the one afternoon, and Jo grazed her hand trying to scoop together one snowball from the top of the garden wall.

Christmas shopping wasn't going to be much fun without Tash. It had been a laugh with her last year, ending in loads of presents bought for each other and hardly anything for anyone else, with no money left to speak of either. This year Jo would have to go on her own. There was always Fizz, but . . . 'I don't think so!' she said, dismissing the idea instantly.

She'd set her heart on a waterwheel for the Blob. If you poured water through the funnel at the top, the plastic buckets on the spokes filled and turned the wheel. The Blob would enjoy playing with it in the bath – this she knew. He loved filling yoghurt pots, and falling water seemed to mesmerise him.

For Tash, Jo had bought a calendar with dogs on it. She could give it to her when she came down to spend Christmas Day with her mum. Seeing Tash again was almost the most exciting thing about Christmas – well, that and Gran, and the presents.

Early on Christmas Eve, Jo phoned Tash's mother. 'Is Tash there?'

'No, she isn't. Is that Jo? Oh, Jo, I was so hoping you might be able to tell me news of her. I was expecting her yesterday, but I've heard nothing. I can't speak to them – not on the phone – and I'm just about tearing my hair out!'

'Oh, don't worry. I'm sure she's all right. I'll let you know if I hear and you phone me if you hear, OK?'

Jo put the phone down in a hurry. Adults in a panic were hard to handle.

'Mum, something must have happened to Tash! Her mum doesn't know where she is.'

'Oh, there's bound to be some simple explanation. She'll turn up!' said her mother cheerfully.

Jo spent the morning fretting as she decorated a papier mâché bowl for her gran.

'Maybe she's ill. Or perhaps she's had an accident and she's lying in a ditch somewhere and nobody knows!'

'Unlikely,' said her mother, spooning mincemeat into pastry cases.

In the afternoon Jo varnished her bowl and in the evening she wrapped it just before her gran arrived, having finished it off with a blast of her mother's hair-drier. Panic about whether the gift would be finished meant less time to worry about Tash.

Jim fetched Gran from the coach station in his van, and Jo accompanied him. What with the hugs and the kisses, helping her gran unpack her bags and listening to her stories of the OAPs in Disneyland Paris, Jo forgot about Tash.

That evening, Gran came up to chat to Jo before she went to sleep. It was the blue of the glass beads round her neck which fell forward as she bent to kiss Jo that triggered the thought. Strange how those little creatures lived in Jo's head, in her memory, forcing themselves into her mind just when she thought she'd forgotten them.

'Gran . . .' she said slowly.

'What is it, pet?'

'Can you keep a secret?'

'I should think I can! My bad memory usually sees to that.' But then, seeing the seriousness of Jo's face, she added, 'What is it? You can tell your old gran.'

Jo spoke quietly, whispering almost. This was so very important to her, and even as she was speaking, she wondered if she should be talking about what she had seen.

'In the river . . . I saw . . . something . . . Blue, like your beads . . . tiny . . . and it sparkled and it had little arms and a head and hair . . . and I don't know what it was, Gran!'

Her gran sat silently, as though waiting for more. Jo held her breath, also waiting.

'My goodness, and here was I thinking you were too old for fairies!' she laughed. 'You'll be needing to get off to sleep right away before Santa Claus comes tumbling down the chimney, won't you!'

Her gran was laughing but Jo didn't feel like smiling. Sad, that was what she felt, let down. She had really thought her gran would have taken her seriously.

Gran leant forward to tuck the duvet under her chin. 'Night night, sleep tight,' she said.

'Mind the bed bugs don't bite,' Jo responded automatically.

For a few minutes she lay there, eyes open, all thoughts of Christmas far away. You're on your own now, kid, she told herself with a sigh. Maybe it's better that way. Least I know now to keep it secret – if Gran didn't believe me, who else would.

And with that thought she rolled on to her side, tucking her knees up under her chin, and went to sleep.

There was no room for anything on Christmas morning except the excitement of present opening. The biggest surprise for Jo was the package from Jim, who gave her a personal stereo and two tapes, with a note which said, 'Thank you for sharing your family,' after which Jo couldn't look at him without blushing. In fact, there was so much to do, what with trying to explain all his new educational toys to a slightly uninterested Blob, that Jo hardly noticed the phone ringing.

Even when her mother said, 'Let me take your number,' and flapped her arms at Jim to signal for paper and pencil, Jo didn't take particular notice.

'Quick, Jo!' her mother called, having written the number on the back of a Christmas card. 'It's for you.'

'Me?' She clambered over the mounds of discarded paper and took the receiver.

'Jo?'

'Tash! Are you all right? I've been so worried!' How could she have let her friend slip out of her thoughts? 'Where are you?'

'In a phone box somewhere in Wales – we're snowed in!'

At that point the beeps cut their conversation short.

It wasn't quite as simple as just calling back, but eventually Jo got the operator to help and the number rang.

'Where've you been? I'm freezing my feet off here!'

'Tash, what happened?'

'Snow happened, that's what! Got snowed in, couldn't get the van out. We shovelled all day, but there's just too much of it. We gave up yesterday.'

'I thought you'd be here last night.'

'So did I.'

'Your mum was frantic!'

'Was she?' Tash didn't sound convinced.

'Got you a present,' Jo said.

'Same here. We had to walk miles to get to the phone.'

'Miles?'

'Well, felt like it. Dad came with me, and the dogs – they're outside now. I had to phone Mum too. There's snow everywhere. You can't believe it. Hey, guess what Dad got me?'

'What?'

'A TV – but the picture's all blurred and he's got to fix the aerial.'

'Are you going to watch the Eddie Murphy?'

'What time?'

'3.20.'

'3.20 – right. Nothing else to do. Think of me at 3.15, right? And I'll think of you.'

'OK. Wish you hadn't got snowed in.'

'Me too.'

'That's long enough, Jo – wish her a Happy Christmas from me,' her mother cut in.

'Mum says Happy Christmas.'

'Thanks – same from me.'

'Yes – and me.'

There was a pause.

'Mum says I've got to go.'

'Yes – Dad's getting mad too.'

'Come down when the snow's gone.'

'OK.'

'Miss you.'

'Me too.'

Finally there was a tiny click as somewhere far away, in that snow-bound phone box, the receiver was replaced in its cradle.

Tash was to come down for New Year's Eve; a postcard of a Welsh woman in a tall black hat told Jo this in the dull week which followed Christmas. Immediately she started to make plans, but it turned out that Tash's mother was insisting she spend the evening at home with her family. She did say Jo was welcome to come and see Tash there, though, which was better than nothing.

It was great to see Tash again, but Jo hadn't counted on so many of her relatives being around too. They had no chance to talk on their own, catch up on all those weeks apart.

The food was good, though. Lots of puddings: trifles and chocolate mousse and luscious lemon cake and no one to make sure you had any first course, and there was Coke to drink.

At ten to midnight, Tash's mum appeared with a tray of champagne and they all had to gather in the living room, put paper hats on and be ready with the party poppers. Tash's Uncle Bob turned on the radio and as Big Ben chimed they all sang 'Auld Lang Syne', holding hands in a circle. Even Grandpa was woken up to join in. Everyone kissed everyone else, and Jo noticed that Tash's mum had to blow her nose hard after she'd kissed Tash.

At ten past twelve everyone started to look for their coats and shoes. Uncle Bob offered to drop Jo off at her house, leaving her and Tash only a few seconds to make arrangements for the next day.

'We'll go to the brook, eh?' Tash suggested. 'I might get to see you know what.'

Jo frowned at her and put her finger to her mouth.

'What are you two plotting?' Tash's mother asked.

'Nothing!'

At that moment there came a sharp ring at the front door.

'Who on earth . . .?' They were all standing in the little hallway, bundled up in coats and scarves. Aunty Bunny, the nearest to the door, opened it and let out a high-pitched scream. There on the doorstep stood a figure in a dark cape and hood, face blacked out. The figure opened its mouth and let rip a blood-curdling, laughing-hyena cry.

'Relax, everyone,' said Tash. 'It's only Fizz!'

Disguise penetrated, he threw back his hood to reveal the familiar striped baseball cap, and put a wad of chewing gum back in his mouth.

'Happy New Year!' he said cheerfully.

'Can I give you a lift home?' asked Uncle Bob rather pointedly.

'Nah, ta. Got my board,' said Fizz.

'See you tomorrow, Fizz,' Tash hissed under her breath. 'We'll come round. OK?'

And as Jo squeezed into the back seat of the car, Fizz jumped on to his board and sped off down the hill, black cloak billowing out behind him.

Unfortunately, Jo didn't even wake up until eleven on New Year's Day. It was so quiet: no traffic from the road; no click-click of people's heels as they marched along the pavements; no sound of milk bottles being delivered. It was as though everyone had died in the night.

In a panic she dialled Tash's number. This was their one precious day together! How could they squander it in sleep? But Tash wasn't awake herself and her mother wouldn't disturb her. By the time Tash eventually arrived at Jo's house, it was lunchtime. Jo's mum put a plate of turkey sandwiches on the table which Tash couldn't resist.

'I'm starving. Missed my breakfast, didn't I?'

The next set-back was her bike. When they wheeled it from the garage where Jim had left it, they discovered it had two flat tyres. The day was cold and foggy, and Jo could feel Tash's enthusiasm waning.

'I've got to be home by five. Dad's coming to collect me,' she warned Jo, who grabbed the pump and started working away with all her strength.

There was Fizz to collect as well, and though Jo felt that this was well beyond the call of duty, Tash insisted that she'd promised. As it happened, they had only made it to the garden gate when, from out of the fog, Fizz emerged.

'Thought you might have called it off,' he said.

'No way!' Jo muttered through gritted teeth.

It was a bleak ride, the cold intensified by swirls of fog which lay heavily in the lungs and made it difficult to breathe. Jo and Tash cycled grimly, heads down, not saying much so as not to waste breath. Fizz had steamed ahead and was on the bridge when they arrived. He'd even had time to build himself a cairn of pebbles on the parapet wall and was about to skim smaller stones at it to knock it down. The mist seemed to be swirling even more densely over the water, almost like steam, so that it was difficult to make anything out from above.

The two girls clambered down the bank and peered more directly into the water, which was brown and dull.

'We'll never see anything on a day like this,' Jo said to Tash. 'I hate New Year's Day. It's a dead day!' So saying, she stomped angrily back to the bridge.

'What's up with her?' she heard Fizz asking Tash.

Jo stood at the far end of the bridge, staring into the water, hearing the plink of stones as Fizz hit his target. Otherwise, there was an eerie silence.

Tash came and stood next to her. 'I do believe you, you know. We'll have better luck next time.

Why don't we go and wish the old man a Happy New Year, eh?'

The day was jinxed. When they got back to their bikes, Tash's back tyre was completely flat again.

'Slow puncture,' Fizz diagnosed as he took out his pump.

It didn't take that long to blow up the tyre, but long enough to rule out a visit to Tom if Tash was to meet her five o'clock deadline. As they cycled past his cottage they waved and called out, but Tom, sitting in his armchair by the stove with a piece of buttered toast, heard and saw nothing.

# 8

*Alone on the rock outside the grooming chamber, Axos and Odol sit on the darker stone, recently exposed, where once the water spilled its force.*

*'It is time!' Axos tells his friend. 'I must tell now what I see in my mind. It will be a Dream of the Future.'*

*It is Axos's dream, but Odol will take the bowl from Anno and give it to Axos. She will stand by her friend and it will be as though it were her dream too. They enter the chamber. Odol does as she plans. There is no surprise in the minds of the elders. They sit meekly, ready to receive.*

*Axos stares into the brackish water at the bottom of the bowl. He stares as he has seen the elders stare. In the surface of the water he sees his own eye appear, and the O in its centre. That is the place to look, he knows. And as he looks, his mind reflects what he sees.*

*'Beyond our world are other worlds. From the Dreams of the Past we know this to be true.' Axos begins hesitantly, but with each thought his confidence and strength grow from conviction.*

*'Behind us are the hills and the mountains, and behind them are more hills and more mountains,*

*and behind them are yet more with no end. In front of us the river winds on down to the sea, and beyond the sea to other seas, and beyond them to other seas and other lands with no end. To the one side and to the other side it is the same: land and water, land and water further than our imaginings. Above is the sky and other worlds that wink and blink possibilities to us from the deep dark of the night. Below us too, are worlds unknown.*

*'We are only what we know. Yet there exists an infinity of knowings. The salmon leaping over our rocks tell us of cool tangy waters where they swim down below us and also of warmer, safer pools above us where they make their nurseries. The eels tell us of the warm salty depths so far away and the vast journeys they travel to reach our waters. The birds that feed here fly away somewhere when they disappear from our world. Even the Paddlefeet let us know of other worlds.*

*'We are not all there is. We know this to be true. This we must hold on to. There is, outside our knowing, something more to know.'*

At the end of the telling, Axos sits transfixed. His mind is turning and tumbling. Instead of following the others into their crowded dreaming, he slips away outside the water curtain to sit on the edge of a pool of stiller water. He is agitated; his thoughts are fragmented, chaotic.

Odol, sensing his disturbance, follows him.

'I do not know what those things are that lie beyond our knowing,' Axos frets to her. 'There are

68

*shapes, but shapes without names. I do not know how it will be, I only know that it is time . . .'*

*'It is . . .'*

*'There will be a way . . .'*

*'There will . . .'*

*'We must be ready, receptive, for it must be soon!'*

Above where the waterfall used to roar, Tom leant over the parapet wall, staring gloomily into the water. He was wheezing rather and his breath hung visibly on the air. All muffled up he was, a knitted hat pulled down over his ears, though according to the calendar this was the first day of spring. Not wearing gloves, though. Didn't believe in them, never had. The skin on his hands was as rough as the stone wall he was leaning on.

Still lower, the water level. Incredible, that this could happen in one man's lifetime! No heron now, his former fishing rival, not clapped eyes on him for many a month. And what was more to the point, no fish. This time, as he leaned over the water, he could see nothing to reassure him. No speckled shadowy shapes, and no flash of blue either.

'I worry for them. I worry for them all,' he said out loud, hunching his shoulders up round his ears.

*Down on the rocks beneath him, Axos and Odol sit. They have brought the newly named Zoy, Mox and Lol to play in the shrinking pool beneath the waterfall.*

'*Do not go beyond the pool!*' *they have been told repeatedly.*

*While they watch, Axos and Odol exchange thoughts. There is an urgency now. Every day they witness their elders fading to colourless ghosts behind the trickle of water which was once their protection. Before, the grooming chamber was full of blue life, now the Waterfolk have shrivelled and desiccated to mere wisps, tricks of the light. Soon they will have vanished altogether, only space remaining where once they were. This Axos and Odol know.*

'*It must come soon. There is not much more time. There must be a way!*' *It is Axos's thought.*

'*Must be.*'

'*I will not give in! I will not fade away!*'

'*Nor I!*'

'*There must be something that will save us. I am ready for the knowing,*' *says Axos.*

In the silence of his own mind, Tom's head was suddenly filled with voices. At first he thought it was that wretched buzzing he'd told the doctor about only last week. 'Like interference on the wireless: a high buzzing and so loud, it drowns out every thing else,' he'd explained. The doctor had checked his blood pressure and given him a bottle of pills which Tom had put on the mantelpiece, unopened.

He tapped the side of his head with his hand, as though trying to knock the sound away. But there it was again. Not the same, though, not buzzing. No, it was voices.

'I am ready for the knowing.'

'As I am.'

It was them. Had to be.

Eager to check with his eyes, Tom scrambled down the bank as quickly as he could in view of his age, the lack of light, and the fact that he was bundled up like a scarecrow. The sound had to come from the rocks beneath the trickle of water, just under where he had been standing on the bridge. Had to. He screwed up his eyes. Maybe there was something: a play of the light, a sense of movement. He couldn't be sure.

'Are you there?' He thought the words as slowly and intensely as he could. 'Are you still there?'

*Axos and Odol catch the words. They move quietly back into the shadows. But on the threshold to the chamber, at the place where the water meets the rock, they pause and stare into each other's eyes.*

*'Paddlefeet!' they say.*

Had anyone been watching they would have seen an old man in a red plaid jacket, face shining with excitement, scrambling up the river-bank, running to the centre of the bridge and leaning far over the parapet as though he were going to nosedive into the river below.

It was Axos's message which Tom received. It was clear and it swept the doubt from his mind.

*'The rains have failed us. The water is failing us. Without it we will perish. We need your help.'*

Tom, hanging upside down, heard those words as clear as a bell.

'I'll help you all I can,' he promised. 'Just tell me what I'm to do.'

But no answer came.

*Below on the rocks, Axos and Odol hear his promise. It is enough. There is no answer to give to his question because there is no knowing.*

And Tom, likewise, hadn't a clue. Not yet.

Whether it was the cold air, or the excitement of hearing those voices again after all those years, or the terrible responsibility which now fell on his shoulders, Tom's breathing was so rough it was hurting his chest and the blood was rushing round his brain like a red tidal wave. Stretching out a hand to steady himself, he found it was shaking. No damn good to anyone like this! he reprimanded himself. Get a grip Tom, lad, get a grip.

It was while he stood there, calming his breath and his thoughts, that he caught another cry – fainter this time, less distinct, but so piercing in its urgency he never even paused for thought. Back over the far side of the bridge he went and along the towpath, retracing his steps, his mind quite clear and focused, like a young dog tracing a scent.

*It is Zoy who leads them. He is the first to venture out of the safety of the pool into the quicker water, to toss and tumble in the bubbling spill where the water current is strongest.*

*And where he leads Lol and Mox follow.*

*In the lower pool the water has a grittier quality.*

Mud churns around them, mud and the soft bodies of countless frogs, manoeuvring for space, searching for room to deposit the eggs bursting from their bodies.

'This I do not like!' whimpers Mox.

'Let's go back,' says Lol, turning to fight her way back through the soft bodies to the water which she knows still falls over the step. Above them somewhere is their home, so very near. If only Odol and Axos were with them now, they would help them to safety.

'Quick! Come this way. I have found a way through,' calls Lol. Mox follows the direction of the thought. Sure enough, by worming and squirming, he finds himself in a little pool of clearer water. Here is Lol. And above them towers the rock face. Together they hug each other and tremble, for they do not know how to return.

And where is Zoy? They call to him. 'Zoy! Zoy! Come to us. We are safe here!' But there is no answer.

Axos, distracted by his thoughts, scans his eye over the pool absently. It takes a second for him to register that the youngers are nowhere in sight.

Instantly, Axos and Odol both dive into the pool. They listen. They look. They turn and twist to left and right. But there is no sign of the youngers. Frantically they dive and surface, scouring the perimeters of the pool, searching under the rocks and amongst the weed.

'If you are hiding, come out,' Axos calls.

There is no answer.

It is only when Odol is peering over the fall into

73

*the lower pool that she catches their weak cries. There is no time to reflect. Axos follows Odol down the fall. They find the terrified youngers and each takes one on his or her shoulders.*

*'Hold on tight!' Odol commands as she struggles to find a way to safety. 'The weed! By the bank!' she says to Axos.*

*Hand over hand, they haul and pull and arrive exhausted in the upper pool, too tired to do more than shake the youngers from their backs. Too terrified to speak, Mox and Lol open their single green eyes in unspeakable misery.*

*'Zoy! Where is Zoy?' Axos asks. The blankness of their reply regenerates him.*

*'Take them back!' he tells Odol, turning once more into the current which whisks him off into the teeming frog nursery.*

Tom had to pause for just a moment by the lower pool to catch his breath. He'd never heard such a racket as was coming from his chest and his heart felt fit to burst. There it was again! Just the faintest of whimpers, but enough to squeeze a last injection of adrenaline into his tired old limbs.

Impossible to see anything, the muddy water all churning and frothy near the sides. Like peering into brown soup. Somehow, he managed to get himself down into a crouching position, the trunk of a goat-willow giving him support. With the edge of the water lapping round the toes of his boots, he peered more deeply into the water. Frogs! Hundreds of them, all scrabbling about, crawling on top of each other, eyes goggling and astonished.

And that's where the sound was coming from, too. So faint now, but from just in front of him. With his bare hands, Tom stirred the water. It was like cold porridge. Horrible! Then he saw it, a tiny blue light trapped deep inside the jellied mass.

'Hold on! I'll get you,' he promised. But he couldn't get hold of it, no matter what. He'd pinch and it would slip away, or he'd bring up his hands, sure he'd got it, only to find himself holding a mass of clear gloop, dotted with black, no sign of the blue at all. The more he tried, the more desperate he became. Gradually he sensed the silence. Not even the softest sound, though he nearly screwed his brain up trying to hear it.

It was hopeless. He was useless. No longer that young boy with a jewel on his braces, just a tired old man with clumsy fingers and aching legs. He straightened himself up slowly and despondently, the lightness in his head seeming to compensate for the heaviness in his boots.

Clutching the tree, waiting to get his breath back, he heard another sound: *Zoy!* It was a piercing call, clear as a bell. As Tom stood there, he saw again, for sure and certain, that flash of blue, quicker than a kingfisher on the wing. It was carried in the water which fell over the little step of rock in front of him.

*Alone on the rock, Odol scans the pool for her friend.*
*Mox and Lol are safe in the chamber behind her.*
*She sees the water ripple, and her heart for one*
*moment leaps excitedly. Then she sees a sadness*
*in Axos's movement, transmitting a message more*
*certain than thought.*

*As he climbs out of the water on to the grey rock,*
*Axos holds the body of Zoy in his arms. Lifeless and*
*limp, and the palest of blues, the colour weeping out*
*of him in the trails of glue which still cling to his*
*body.*

So tired Tom felt that evening, so very tired,
and no surprise in that. Cavorting about like a
teenager! But his brain was tired too, and his
mind. He didn't want to think any more about
the voices he had heard, the promises he had
made and the thing that he had not been able
to do.

'They chose the wrong person,' he muttered
to Toby, who lay heavily in front of the dying
fire.

He should put another log on to keep them
both warm through the evening. He should put
the kettle on too and maybe the light. The
thoughts never seemed to reach his limbs,
though. So there he sat. He was only alerted
when the little clock on the mantelpiece struck
half past something. He lifted his head to see half
past what – not that it mattered – and then he
caught sight of it. The envelope, and written on

it in large distinct letters: JO – 24 TRELAWNY GARDENS.

Last chance. Had to! Whatever it took. No paper within reach – just the Christmas card from the vicar still on display. Fortunately the stubby pencil was still where he had left it, by the envelope.

'Jo,' he wrote. 'They need help. I know you know what. Tom.'

# 9

As it happened, Jo wasn't the only one who was interested in water. Jim turned out to know a considerable amount about pondlife, and Jo's mum had volunteered him at the last PTA meeting to clear out and replant the neglected school pond – much to Jo's surprise and embarrassment.

The first time Jim went to make a 'recce' of the pond, Jo declined to go with him. When he got back, she was sitting on the back step making a whistle out of a blade of grass.

'Some pond you've got there,' he told Jo as he padded into the kitchen in his thick Norwegian socks. 'Choked, utterly choked. I began the clearing – I think we should tear everything out and start again. I'll go up again next Saturday. Are you coming?'

'Maybe,' Jo said.

And on that very Saturday morning, the card arrived for Jo.

'Letter for you,' her mother said, skimming the brown envelope across the kitchen like a frisbee.

Jo's heart leapt. Must be from Tash! Then she recognised her own handwriting. She turned the envelope over carefully.

'Who's it from?' her mother asked.

Written on the back were these words: 'Forwarded by Reverend Fred Bacon, All Hallows Church, Littleham on the Ooze.'

There was something he had tried to scribble out. Jo peered at it. '4 × 2″ brass screws.'

She slit the envelope open with her index finger and inside was a Christmas card, folded to fit.

'A Christmas card! Bit on the late side,' her mother commented. 'We're well into spring now.'

Jo turned her back on her mother to read the card. 'They need help. I know you know what. Tom.'

She read the message a second time but it didn't make any more sense. 'They need help . . .' Who exactly?

She stood up suddenly. 'I have to go out to see Tom, the old fisherman,' she announced. 'He needs help.'

Her mother looked at her suspiciously. 'What kind of help?'

'Don't know – doesn't say.'

'Well, I'm not happy about that at all. I don't know anything about this man, as I've told you before, Jo.'

'Jim's met him!' Jo protested.

'That's as maybe,' her mother said, 'but I'm

not having you going out there on your own. If you've got to go, take Fizz or someone. And you can't go today, anyway – you promised to help Jim at the pond.'

And before Jim could open his mouth to say he wasn't bothered she added, 'And that's the end of the matter.'

It was so annoying the way her mother always got the last word. It left Jo boiling inside, as though she wanted to scratch and scratch but at places she couldn't reach. Upstairs, she pinched hard at the toothpaste so that it shot out of the tube in a curl of surprise. White, this new lot, with one stripe of clear blue. It caught the light and then coiled back on itself, piercing Jo's mind, spearing through the memory of the river sighting, the fishing float on Tom's kitchen table, the colour of Tom's eyes, and the way he looked at her.

'I will come, Tom,' she whispered as she spat into the bowl. 'As soon as I can . . . I'll help if I can.' She turned the tap and water gushed the swirl of frothy toothpaste away.

'Ready when you are, Jo,' Jim called. 'That pond needs us!'

In his thigh-length waders, Jim did most of the work at the pond, clawing out the tangled weeds and throwing them on to the bank, from where Jo, somewhat distractedly, loaded them into a wheelbarrow. Jim had brought a thermos and some pieces of fruit cake and they sat together, back to back on a plastic carrier bag, their protection against the damp grass.

Jim was busy hatching his plans for the pond. He was used to Jo's lack of communication as far as he was concerned, and it didn't bother him as much as it did Jo's mum.

'I think we're nearly ready to introduce new plants. I thought some oxygenators first, like curled pond weed. Then, when we're established, we'll think about some marginals: cuckoo flower, some water mint, brooklime . . . And then we'll be ready to introduce the first little creatures. You'd be amazed, though – most of them will arrive all on their own.

But Jo was hardly listening to him. She had her mind fastened on another plan altogether. Over the far side of the pond where the water fed into it, draining the school field, she had a sudden intense vision: running water, gushing and splashing with vigour and life.

'Could we make a proper waterfall over there?' She cut across Jim's planning.

'What? Where?'

Jo jumped up and went over to the broken drainpipe which was spilling its contents into the pond beneath.

Jim joined her. 'I don't see why not. You could clear the pipe out, for a start.'

A few feet back, the pipe was completely clogged with a mulch of soggy brown leaves; water dribbled down the sides, turning the grass beneath into a swamp. With far greater enthusiasm than before, Jo started to clear it out. The first time she plunged her hand into the cold and soggy mess, she grimaced – but once wet and dirty and smelling of drains, the worst was over and she began to enjoy what she was doing. Satisfying it was, too, turning the sluggish trickle into a fast-moving flow.

'There's a couple of broken sections,' she told Jim as he came over to inspect her work.

'Soon replace them,' he told her. 'Come on, that's enough for one day. I'm starving!'

Later that evening, her mother safely occupied in the bathroom hosing the remains of the day from the Blob, Jim sitting in the living room reading his *Pond Life*, Jo slipped out of the back door. By the time she had returned, her mother was coming down the stairs carrying the alphabet bathtowel. Inside it was the Blob, whose current joke was hiding. Jo saw her opportunity while everyone was pretending to wonder where he was.

'I'm going taddying tomorrow, Mum, OK? We'll need tadpoles for our pond, won't we?' she asked Jim.

'Indeed,' he agreed. 'Whoever heard of a pond without tadpoles?'

'And it's all right, I don't need a lift out to the river. Fizz is coming with me. I already asked him,' she added hurriedly before her mother could say anything.

Fizz met Jo in the usual place the following

morning. The chestnut tree was smothered in pink blossoms like candelabras. Its leaves were so fresh they were lime green where they'd broken out of their sticky casings.

With a faster bike and longer legs, Fizz tore off in front of Jo, only stopping outside the old man's gate to wait for her. A couple of smoothly dressed men in suits were walking down the path and looked suspiciously at him. A white Vauxhall Cavalier was parked off the lane by the hedge.

Jo came panting into view. Having gained some speed, she didn't want to waste the opportunity to get ahead of Fizz.

'Let's stop and show him the taddies on the way back,' she called as she whizzed past.

She had hatched her plan carefully. Without Fizz her mother would not have let her come to visit Tom, but there was no way she wanted him involved in her mission. It was her and Tom, just the two of them. She'd go down to the river with Fizz, get him taddying, then find an excuse to leave him there while she sneaked back to have a word with Tom and find out what this was all about.

They parked their bikes next to the weeping willow tree; its stringy arms were on the point of erupting into silver green.

'Oh no!' Jo did nothing to conceal her horror.

The two stared in disbelief. The pool beneath the waterfall, formerly such a rich hunting ground for tadpoles, was barely more than a muddy puddle. The waterfall itself was now a paltry trickle, a mere tap flow across, the water only moving at the pace of a tap with a faulty washer.

'I can't believe this is happening,' Jo muttered.

Fizz was clambering down the bank in front of her. 'It's OK,' he called back to her. 'Still loads of tadpoles.'

Indeed, the water was heaving with them.

'It's *all* tadpole in fact,' Jo said. 'Not much water.'

Fizz had hunkered down and was busy poking at the seething mass with a stick.

'Leave it out!' Jo said crossly. 'You'll hurt them.'

With that inducement, Fizz managed to grasp a particularly fat tadpole by the tail between his finger and thumb. He stood up and advanced towards Jo, dangling it in front of her nose.

'Cut it out, Fizz!' She recalled the maggots and swallowed down her desire to scream and to slap him across the face.

'Get the jar!' she ordered him. 'Take as many as you can.' She turned away and started scooping up as many as possible herself. 'Let's take lots. They'll stand a better chance in the pond.'

They filled their jars to the brim, a jellied black mass of small bodies and thrashing tails.

Jo couldn't stop thoughts from flooding into her mind. Where would the frogs go? And what about next year? Would there be any more taddying expeditions? She couldn't, she just couldn't, leave Fizz to this mercy mission – they'd have to go together. Perhaps this was what Tom meant. 'They need your help.' The tadpoles certainly needed help!

'Let's go and see Tom,' Jo suggested, trying not to look at the dried rocks where the waterfall used to gush. 'Let's show him the taddies.'

They tied string carefully round the rims of their jars and looped them over the handlebars. Even though Jo tried to cycle as smoothly as she could, at one bump in the road the bike gave a lurch and she lost a couple of casualties. She hated the thought of them gasping and squirming on the hard tarmac. But by the time she came to a gentle halt, there came a whoop from Fizz behind her.

'Yeah! Got 'em!'

Jo screeched with horror. 'What did you do?' she shrieked – but she knew.

'Put 'em out of their misery!' Fizz called out cheerfully and sped on past her. Jo couldn't bear to look. In a fury, she clambered back on her bike and went after him.

Fizz, reaching the cottage before she did, swung in through the open gate and cycled up to the tree where he stopped, waiting for her. Jo got off at the gate and wheeled her bike over to him.

'How could you, Fizz! We're meant to be saving them!'

'Hey! What are you kids doing?' A van had

drawn up behind them at the gate and a burly man was climbing out of the driver's seat.

From out of the rear of the van, he pulled a pole with a 'For Sale' board at the end. Jo and Fizz exchanged glances. Then, not really concerned about the children, the man chose his spot by the gate, jumped up on to the stepladder which he'd placed there, and proceeded to bang down on the top of the pole with a large mallet.

'Is Tom moving?' Jo asked him nervously.

'He's moved already!' the man chuckled.

'Where?'

'Down the road.' The man jerked his thumb over his shoulder. 'See the steeple?'

Jo nodded.

'That's where he's moved to – the graveyard.'

'What!'

'No – I shouldn't tease.' The man tested his pole, folded up the steps and came over to where she was standing. 'Friend of his, were you?'

'I s'pose so.'

'Sorry to say, he passed on a few weeks ago, I understand. Found him sitting in his chair. The fire was still warm, apparently.'

'What about Toby?'

'The dog? You knew him? Well, he was warm too, they said – but I guess he gave up when he sensed the old man had given up on him. Happens like that, they say.'

'Poor Toby! Poor Tom!' Jo felt a sob rising in her throat.

'Aye, well – he were a ripe old age.'

Tears were running down Jo's face.

The burly man shifted uneasily. 'Now don't you take on. He had a good innings – they both did.'

Fizz's attention seemed to be suddenly focused on a couple of blue tits squabbling in the branches above his head. He took the end of his gum between finger and thumb and pulled a long thread of grey, then threw back his head and sucked it back in like a fisherman reeling in his line.

'We were going to show him our tadpoles,' Jo sobbed.

The man cleared his throat. In a softer tone, he said, 'Been taddyin', have you? Well, he'd have liked that. A river man all his life, was Tom.'

Jo sniffed savagely, her sobbing suddenly controlled by an awful thought. What had Tom meant? She'd never know now! And no one would know that she didn't know. And she'd never be able to help whatever it was, unless Tom had meant the tadpoles, and she knew deep down that he hadn't. There was nothing she could do, nothing except sob again.

'Well . . .' The man shifted the weight of the mallet to his other hand and coughed nervously. 'I got to be moving on – few more signs I got to put up. Do it in my own time see, Sundays, for the agents. Drive the dustcart in the week.'

He drove off towards the church, leaving Jo and Fizz in the quiet of Tom's garden.

'How could he go and die just now?' Jo blurted out. 'Why couldn't he have waited a bit longer!' She banged her fists against the old Bramley tree with frustration.

Fizz shrugged awkwardly. 'He was dead old,' he said.

There was nothing to linger for. They tied the jars of tadpoles on to their handle bars and set off slowly down the lane. At All Hallows, Jo slowed her bike to a halt.

'I think I'll just go and see . . . You don't have to come,' she added hastily.

'I'll hold the bike,' Fizz volunteered.

It wasn't difficult to find the grave, the only new mound of freshly turned clay, ugly and pale in this quiet, green place. There was no name on the simple wooden cross. On the top of the mound there was a single wreath of wilting flowers with a card attached. The letters, though faded, were still legible and Jo recognised the handwriting from the back of the envelope: 'Tom. A river man. With you dies much wisdom. Fondly, Fred and Clare Bacon.'

There was nothing more, though what she'd expected, Jo couldn't have said. Inside her head, she sent one last urgent plea to the man she still saw in his red plaid jacket, woolly hat on his head, eyes blue and full of life.

'I will help if I can, but I don't know what

I'm meant to be helping! You got me ready but why didn't you tell me what for!'

She could feel the tears pricking the backs of her eyes. She didn't want to cry again.

'Anyway,' she added as an afterthought. 'I'm more angry than sad, you know!'

With that reprimand she turned and walked purposefully back to Fizz.

They cycled side by side but in silence for the first little while.

'Did they put the old dog in with him?' Fizz asked finally.

'Don't know. Can you bury dogs in church-yards?' Jo said.

'Don't see why not.'

'Nor do I.'

*Where the light has penetrated their chambers and dried the skin of the rock to a pale chalky mauve, the smoke-like streaks of the other Waterfolk have thinned to fine gossamer threads before vanishing completely. Even Nonno, the Giver of Names, has gone. There will be no more names for him to give.*

*Anno, the Keeper of the Circle, is the last elder to disappear. From where he lies on the rock floor, his body curved like a shadow round the edges of the circle he guards, he sees the future in Axos and it comforts him.*

*For some time, Axos, and Odol have chosen not to enter the chamber because of the emptiness there. Their days are spent searching out moisture, in crev-ices, trapped between strands of matted weed, caught* in shadowy places, replenished by morning dew. They use the energy they find to think forward, not back where shadows lie.

One evening, however, Axos receives a faint calling of his name. It comes from the grooming chamber. It is a call he must respond to. Leaving Odol to care for the youngers, he retreats into the chamber. The rock is dry as bone. There, in the furthest recess beyond the circle, is the place where the call has come from.

'It is my time of going. Anno's circle has turned. Your time is still to come. This is how it is. But before I vanish I will charge you, Axos, to be the Keeper of the Circle. Inside the circle you will find the truth. You must remember this, Axos, and when it is your turn, when your circle is completed, you must pass this office on as I have done.'

The thoughts are like whispers, yet Axos feels their power. He hangs his head.

'There is no water in the bowl,' Anno continues. 'Fill it, Axos!'

It is the last thought that Axos catches. All is silent. He does not look, for there is nothing to see. He will carry Anno's words inside himself with care, for they are weighty and precious.

In the far recesses of a rock crevice, Odol sits, curled under a small clump of green moss. Mox and Lol are protected in her lap, mere wisps of brown under the green. They are the sole remaining Waterfolk.

Axos joins them, but he does not tell of his meeting with Anno. He chooses to speak of the future.

'They were here again.'

'Plundering the frog nursery,' says Odol.

Axos and Odol still have the light within them. They may continue to exchange thoughts – just.

'They know,' says Axos.

'The Paddlefeet?'

'Yes.'

' "Not much water." Those are the words I caught,' says Odol.

'They know the tadpoles will die.'

'They will take as many as they can.'

'They are our hope,' says Axos.

'They may take us.'

'That we may live!'

# 10

In the middle of July it rained – massively. So dark was it when Jo opened her eyes, she thought it must be the middle of the night. She turned over and shut them again until a crack of thunder woke her, loud as a pistol shot in her ears, and sheet lightning lit the room strangely, like a flickering strobe light.

There followed a furious wind which battered the trees in the road, breaking off minor branches and hurling them into the street. Then the rain started. It fell in a solid sheet, pouring down the windows like glue, quickly flooding gutters and drainpipes and spilling on to the ground in fountains. The baked earth was so shocked by the virulence of the attack that it seemed unable to accept what was on offer. How it needed that rain! But instead of being sucked down thirstily, the water seemed to bounce back off the surface or lie in ever-deepening lakes.

The rain didn't last long, and although it beat all records for the amount of water falling in two hours in July, it seemed to cause more damage than it gave help. The TV news that evening was filled with pictures of flooding, burst water pipes, traffic jams and roofs blown off by the violent wind.

Next day, Saturday, Jo woke early to a clear blue sky. She had to go back to the river, see what the rain had done. Just be there, ready. Before her mother and Jim had even appeared, she heard the Blob complaining loudly, telling them it was high time they were up and feeding him. Jo scribbled a note: 'Gone fishing', and left it propped against the fruit bowl on the kitchen table. That much she dared, though not to defy her mother's ruling and go alone, whatever the temptation.

She clipped her rod to her bike, put the floats in her saddle bag and cycled off to Fizz's house. As usual the house looked deserted, but as she approached, she saw the postman walking down the garden path, shaking his head.

'I'm not signing nothing!' a thin woman in a pink nightdress called after him, greying hair pulled back from her bony face. She slammed the door furiously, leaving Jo uncertain what to do. She'd never seen Fizz's mum before.

She did as Fizz would have done. Not leaving her bike but straddling it at the gate, or where the gate should have been, she put her fingers in her mouth and gave a piercing whistle. Fizz's head appeared at the window on her second attempt and he was with her, on his bike, fully dressed, two minutes later.

'Do you sleep in your clothes?' Jo asked, but

he was ahead of her and out of earshot, or pretending to be.

Round the corner, he was dawdling, waiting for her to catch him up. 'Where we going?' he asked.

'Fishing,' Jo replied.

That turned out to be a vain hope, though fishing had never been her real reason for the trip. Even after the flash rains of the previous day, there was no river restored and gushing, though perhaps the dark streak in the very centre of the river-bed was a little more sticky, a darker, wetter brown than the surrounding mud.

Fizz, eager to be active, set off exploring the boulders which until so recently had formed the waterfall. The warm dry hollows made excellent toe and hand holds. With his hands grasping the smooth lip of the rock above his head, his toes fumbled for purchase. As he dug in to a deep recess, his foot seemed to crunch on pebbles. Without glancing down, he scuffed them aside to make a smoother surface. Had he listened, he might have heard the chink of pebble on rock, and had he looked he might have seen a cascade of tiny pearl-like stones tumbling over the boulders, their seams of crystal catching the light.

Jo picked herself a long reed from the bank and clambered down across the crisped, flaky earth mosaic to the edge of the darker mud. It smelt dank, fetid almost, warm and suffocating to breathe. Squatting down, she poked her reed into its softness, testing its depth. There was no resistance, she found. Round her head, flies hummed; a big blue dragonfly hovered near where she crouched before dipping and rising away downstream.

Under the protection of a slimy trail of green weed, she was delighted to find some little frogs no bigger than her thumbnail, but perfect, moist and shiny as jelly. She covered them up again quickly.

'I wonder what they're thinking?'

She uncovered them again, just for a second, to look at their quivering throats and tiny black eyes, like drops of ink.

'What are you thinking?' she addressed them directly, urgently, but silently. 'Do you wonder where the water's gone? Where all those other frogs have gone? What's going to happen to you?'

Carefully, she laid the protective weed back over them.

Another thought came to her, clear as clear.

*'Help us! You must help us – before we fade away. We are down here in the cracked earth!'*

The shock of the voice knocked Jo backwards on to the mud. The hair on the back of her neck prickled and her heart was beating so fast she thought she was going to faint. It was as though she was wearing headphones, the sound received in the very middle of her head. It had not come from outside, of that she was sure. They were real words, though, and they came from something real, right under the earth somewhere.

'What? . . . Where? . . . Who?' As she uttered the words, simultaneously she understood. This was it. This was what she had to be ready for.

Carefully, brow furrowed in concentration, Jo probed the cracks near her feet with the long reed. 'I'm coming. Wait! I'm sticking this reed down all the cracks. I'll be very careful – I don't want to stab you – but tell me as soon as you feel anything.'

There was nothing. Her mind was a blank. Quickly, she withdrew her reed. 'Oh no! Have I killed you? Are you there? Say something!'

*'We are here – waiting. There is a darkness above us – like night, but weighty – and a pressure in the earth.'*

Jo quickly shifted her feet from under where she was crouching. 'Are you down there?' Gently, she lowered her probe into a small S-shaped crack beneath her.

*'Yes – yes!'*

'Can you see it?'

*'We can feel it – something near us, above us. We can feel it!'*

'Is it dark? Can you see anything?'

*'We see nothing.'*

Until that moment, Jo realised she had been thinking of frogs, bulbous eyes protruding from their heads.

*'No, not frogs.'*

'What, then?' she responded, without pausing to wonder how her thoughts had reached them.

'*Waterfolk, from behind the waterfall. You have no thought, no picture yet – perhaps you do not know us.*'

Suddenly, Jo saw again the flash of blue, the glass beads, the look in old Tom's eye. 'I do know you. At least, I think I do,' she said slowly.

'What ya' doing?' Fizz suddenly materialised behind her.

It was the second shock inside a couple of minutes. He hadn't intended to make her jump but if he had, he couldn't have done a better job. She screamed, fell over backwards, then got to her feet in a frenzy, pushing his shoulders so he nearly fell himself.

'Get back! Don't stand there!' she screamed at him.

'What's wrong with you?'

'You and your big feet . . . Just get out, can't you!'

Fizz shuffled back, looking anxiously at his feet for snakes or venomous spiders.

Jo bit her lip in agitation. 'Look, sorry, Fizz. Sorry I shouted, you just gave me a fright. Could you go away now!' she said, emotion barely controlled in her voice. 'I want to be . . . I mean, I'm just collecting something . . . It's a secret,' she ended lamely.

Fizz shrugged and turned back to the boulders where he had been climbing. He picked up a flat pebble from habit, holding it ready to skim and bounce across the water surface, forgetting there was only mud. Where could he throw it? Could he reach Jo with it, maybe?

He half-turned to see what she was up to. Crouching intently on the mud, poking a fresh reed into the earth, she was presenting a good target! Fizz hesitated, then dropped the stone, feeling virtuous.

'Are you there?' Jo spoke the thought inside her head. She did not want Fizz to hear her.

'*We are,*' came their weak reply.

'I'll help you. Don't worry.' She directed the thought urgently. 'I'll think of something. I'll get you out!'

'What ya' looking at?' Fizz, curious, had crept up behind her.

This time Jo didn't move. She couldn't. She didn't raise her voice, either. She took a deep breath, just enough time to weigh the possibilities: tell Fizz now, or walk away and leave the Waterfolk, ignoring their cries for help, and come back later, alone, when it would probably be too late.

'I'll have to tell you,' Jo said. 'But you are not to hurt them!' She had wheeled round and hissed at him with such ferocity, Fizz was taken aback.

'I won't,' he promised, 'whatever they are.'

'Slit your throat?'

Fizz made the sign, slicing his hand across his bare skin.

Jo gave him a long hard stare before turning

away. 'There's something down there,' she said quietly, pointing at the crack in the mud.

'What?'

'Shhh! I can't hear them. You've got to keep quiet!'

Fizz, uncertain, stood behind her, eyes nervously scanning the earth.

'*Water . . . fast . . . or we will perish!*'

'Did you hear?' Jo asked him.

'Hear what?' Fizz came closer.

'Just keep quiet. Listen!'

'*We must have water!*'

'Who said that?' Fizz jumped back in surprise.

'*We did.*'

'Who?' Fizz said. 'What's going on?' he asked Jo nervously.

'Sshh! Keep listening,' she said.

'Who's talking?' asked Fizz, confused.

'*We are Waterfolk, from behind the waterfall.*'

'The waterfall? It's all dried up, mate. Gone. Vamooshed!'

'*Just so. As have all the Waterfolk. Only we remain. Help us.*'

Fizz and Jo exchanged glances. 'What are they, these water thingies? What do they look like?'

Jo shrugged. 'Don't know.'

'Can't you see them?' he asked.

Jo shook her head. 'I can just hear them, like you.'

Fizz hunched down beside Jo and peered into the deep crack in the earth. He frowned, took off his cap and wiped his fist over his forehead, sniffing loudly before replacing it.

'*We need water quickly*!' came the plea.

'I've got my water bottle,' Fizz suggested, 'but it's empty.'

'Or there's my sandwich box. We could fill it with water.'

'Where from?'

'I know – what about Tom's place? Oh no,' Jo said, remembering, 'it'll be locked up.'

Fizz tapped the side of his nose. 'No problem.'

There was no time to question, just accept the offer.

'Let's go,' Fizz shouted, already halfway up the bank.

'We'll be back,' Jo promised before following.

They biked to Tom's house to save time, cramming sandwiches into their mouths as they went.

When they arrived, Fizz took command. 'Watch the road, Jo. If anyone comes, just whistle. Won't be long!'

It was just after Jo had heard the tinkling of broken glass that she registered the sound of a car pulling up and a car door opening – an estate agent with a prospective customer. Bad timing. She put her fingers in her mouth but her throat was dry, and though she blew, no sound came. There wasn't time to try again.

She had to think fast. Before the party reached the gate, the estate agent leading the way in his smart suit with a middle-aged couple following, she threw herself on to the ground and started to roll from side to side, moaning loudly and clutching her stomach.

'My goodness!' exclaimed the husband, running over to her. 'Are you all right? We'd better phone for a doctor.'

'There's no phone here!' the estate agent apologised. 'Of course, it would be easy to have one installed. Just one simple phone call . . .'

At that very moment, Fizz appeared round the corner of the house, throwing his fist in the air and shouting triumphantly, 'Yee-ha! Let's go!'

The three adults stared at him aghast. While they were still stunned, Jo scrambled to her feet, picked up her bike and scooted down the road after Fizz as fast as she could.

'What did you have to go and break the glass for?' she shouted breathlessly after him.

'How else did you expect me to get in?'

'Why didn't you slip something down the side of the door?'

'It was a mortice lock, dummy! Last time I use you as a look-out.'

'My mouth went all dry. Anyway, we got the water,' Jo pointed out.

It was surprisingly difficult to relocate the exact spot they'd heard the voices; all the cracks seemed to look the same. It was difficult too to sharpen and focus their minds which were speeding with recent adventures and excitement, their thoughts fragmented, insubstantial.

'Where are you?' Jo said. 'Concentrate!' she told Fizz, who was leaping on and off the boulders on to the dry river-bottom.

Fizz adjusted his cap and screwed up his face before joining her. 'Giving me brain-ache,' he muttered.

Somehow, by squeezing all other extraneous thoughts from their minds, the words started to come through more distinctly. It was like fine-tuning a radio.

'*Here. We are here.*'

'This is it! I remember now.'

Carefully, Jo slipped the reed into the crack at her feet.

'Just hold on . . . We'll take you somewhere where there is plenty of water. You'll like it! The school pond,' she added for Fizz's benefit, as the creatures seemed to catch the images of the new waterfall and the free-flowing water in her mind.

'*This will be a suitable place.*'

'Can you feel this? Can you hold on to it somehow?' Jo wriggled a fresh reed down the crack in front of her.

'*We are holding on to something – be careful, please.*'

Slowly, centimetre, by centimetre, Jo drew up the reed. On the very bottom, curled round each other and clinging to the reed, were two tiny creatures, no bigger than the Blob's little finger. In the bright light, they were so transparent, they seemed almost colourless.

Jo gasped in delight. 'Look!'

Fizz stood behind her. There was a nervousness in his voice. 'What are they? Bugs? Watch out, they might bite!'

Jo shook her head. 'Aren't they beautiful!'

Fizz nodded slowly. They certainly were.

In the warm sunlight, however, the creatures seemed to be fading in front of their eyes. As she saw their translucency, Jo's excitement changed to fear. She was holding a mystery on the point of extinction, a light which might blow out on her breath. The responsibility was agonizing.

*'Water – quickly, please!'*

Immediately Jo submerged the tiny things, still clinging to the reed end, in the sandwich box. Wriggling free, they parted and assumed two distinct miniature shapes. They swam on their backs, their nearly transparent limbs turning blue in front of the children's eyes and, as the colour flooded their bodies, so they each opened a single green eye. It was only when they flicked their tails and rose to the surface Jo noticed the miniscule creatures clinging to their backs: even smaller, paler, with their eyes closed by a silken skin.

'Babies!' Jo squeaked.

*'Yes, precious ones. They must be saved! You must help us. Take us to this place behind a waterfall, a safe place where we may build a new home. The water falling will give us protection and cool our chambers. Behind its safety we may live and dream and tell our tales.'*

'We'll try! Won't we, Fizz?' said Jo.

Fizz nodded.

'*We have water now, but we will need a place where we may rest out of the water also.*'

'I know – like tadpoles,' said Jo.

'*We are not like tadpoles,*' said one of the creatures. '*We may breathe through our skins under the water, or through these places on our faces above the surface. When we swim they close.*'

Jo examined the tiny face that was turned to her. Beneath the solemn green eye were two slits, pinched now and barely visible.

'We could put something in the box for you to climb out on to,' offered Jo. 'Find something, Fizz!' she ordered.

Fizz looked around him. A stick, a lump of mud? What? He stooped and picked up a little pearl-like pebble, lying on the mud at his feet, which caught the light. It looked about the right size. He dropped it into the water with a plink.

'*This is good,*' came the unexpected resonse from the Waterfolk. '*It comes from our circle. We will be happy now to be in the water with the stone from our circle with us. Take us to this place you have in your mind – to this new waterfall. Take us now so we may make a new dwelling and start a new circle.*'

# 11

School grounds were officially off limits at the weekends, not counting the pond development squad who had special permission to visit. If asked what she was doing there, Jo could always plead Jim had given his say-so. Leaving their bikes behind the hedge, she and Fizz sneaked through a much-trampled gap and ran over to the far side of the pond. There was no stone behind the waterfall, just the mud bank of the pond and a straggle of thick grasses. But maybe if Jo and Fizz bent the grasses down and made a kind of nest for the Waterfolk, they could adapt.

Gently, Jo prized the lid from the sandwich box, gasping at the miraculous creatures. In *her* sandwich box! She, Jo, was taking part in a real live fantasy adventure!

'I can't believe it,' she whispered. 'Pinch me, someone!'

'Ow!' she snapped when Fizz obliged. 'Shh, they're saying something.' She lowered her head over the box to concentrate more fully.

'*We wish to be taken out of here!*'

'*This is not to our liking.*'

'*There has been much turbulence.*'

Jo saw the expression on Fizz's face, but before he could voice his indignation she said quickly, 'Fizz, get us a leaf or something to scoop them out with.'

There was one water lily, recently planted by Jim, just within reach. Before Jo could stop him, Fizz had leant forward and snapped a leaf off.

'Not the water lily!' she shouted.

'What?'

'Oh, never mind! Here, give us it.'

The leaf was so large, Jo had to bend it to scoop it into the box, but it served its purpose well. The exhausted Waterfolk hauled themselves out and lay quivering on its shiny surface.

'Hold tight,' Jo told them as she lifted them carefully through the air and round the side of the waterfall, passing the sandwich box to Fizz as she did so. She held the leaf behind the water for a minute or two and then withdrew it. The Waterfolk had gone.

'OK?' she asked. No reply. 'I said, is everything all right?'

Again, no reply. Jo stood uncertainly for a moment, fighting with feelings of disappointment and anti-climax before Fizz pulled her arm.

'Come on! They'll be fine.'

Without thinking, Fizz threw the contents of the box – water and pebble – in an arc over the pond. It caught a rainbow in its curve before falling away into the brown water.

Jo gasped. 'You shouldn't have done that,' she

cried. 'That's their stone! I was going to put it behind the waterfall for them.'

'Too late,' said Fizz. 'I didn't know, did I?'

Just as well, as Jo later pointed out to Fizz, that she wasn't always in such a hurry as he was. If she hadn't lingered while he charged off ahead, who knows what might have happened. As it was, she was just in time to see a movement by the fence in the corner of the field. She stopped in her tracks. Was she mistaken? No, it was a movement in the greenery, definitely. A boy stuck his head out and beckoned to the another. Alarmingly, they had nets, sieves and jamjars in their hands.

'Fizz!' she hissed. But it was too late; she just caught sight of his cap bobbing along behind the hedge. She was on her own.

Back behind the safety of the hedge, she crouched beside her bike. Her heart was beating uncomfortably. The two kids began their dipping, their backs to her, shielding her view of their specimen jars. Actually, she knew from inside information, there wasn't much in the pond to dip as yet beyond the taddies.

With sinking heart, Jo saw the boys' bodies straighten as they peered into one of the sieves. One of the two pulled out a straggle of green weed and threw it back in the water, but there was something else left behind. She saw the other poke at it with a finger and then recoil. Did she hear it or did she just imagine it, that tiny moan of protest? Had it even come from her own lips?

A jamjar was filled with water and then held up; the contents of the sieve were knocked into it; the jamjar was held aloft again against the strong light. It wasn't taddies they were looking at; Jo would have been able to see their dark shapes. Then, to her delight, the boys put the jamjar down on the grass beside them and turned again to the task of dipping.

Jo had to do something. Using her elbows, she crept forward on her tummy, as furtively as a stalking cat. There wasn't far to crawl, and the boys were deeply absorbed. She got right up behind them, close enough to hear their breathing. One had hayfever and kept sniffing. She stretched out her hand.

It all happened in a split-second: grabbing the jar, leaping up, turning and racing back to her bike. It would take the boys a crucial second to come out of shock. They'd give chase, course they would. And they did, shouting and cursing her, but she was away pedalling like a demon, the jar clasped to her shirt front, cold water splashing over her knees.

Not until she reached the safety of her own front garden did she stop and examine the jar. They were there, blue in the murky water.

'You all right?' she asked breathlessly, then wished she hadn't.

'*No! We are very disturbed by sudden storms and*

*wild winds. You promised us peace,*' one of the creatures reproached her.

'I promised nothing,' Jo muttered to herself. 'Don't worry, Plan B. I'll think of something,' she added with a conviction she didn't quite feel.

She propped her bike up against the garage in the front garden and tiptoed down the side of the house. Her mother was sprawled with the Blob on a tartan rug in the garden, as she had predicted. Jim was sitting in a deckchair reading the paper.

'Hi, Mum, I'm back. Desperate for the loo!' she called out as she whizzed into the kitchen and up the stairs.

The Blob's waterwheel! The very thing! In the centre of the wheel, near the pivotal mechanism, there was a small red plastic shelf. The Waterfolk could sit there while the water from above turned the plastic paddles.

After a quick peep out of the window, where she saw her mother carrying a tray of iced tea into the garden, Jo turned to the jam jar. The two creatures, though a brighter blue, were floating on the surface of the water, listlessly, like bloated bodies. The babies were tucked under their chins like water-wings.

'Are you all right?' she asked again anxiously, regretting her lack of sympathy before.

Their replies were weak. '*We need food.*'

'Oh dear, I hadn't thought of that. What do you eat?' Jo asked anxiously.

'*No, no – it is not for you to provide our dreams.*'

'Dreams? I thought you said you were hungry.'

'*Dreams will satisfy. They are our food.*'

'That's handy.' For a moment Jo imagined a life freed from sandwich-making. But on second thoughts: no ice-cream, no strawberries, or crisps, or garlic mayonnaise . . .

'*We are not catching you.*'

'Oh, sorry. I'll try something else. First, I've got to get you out. Just hold on a tick, I'll fetch Mum's slotted spoon.'

Taking the stairs two at a time, Jo leapt back down to the kitchen and returned, panting, with the spoon. 'This should work. I'll scoop you out, and I promise to be careful.'

As though she were draining peas, she raised the Waterfolk up out of the water. As the drops fell from their bodies, so the colour seemed to drain out of them and they turned from that electric blue to turquoise. They sat clinging to the chrome surface of the spoon and stared around them with their huge green eyes.

Next, Jo carried them over to the waterwheel. 'Climb on to that platform and just stay there for a moment.'

Tentatively they did so and sat like builders on a derrick, clinging to the red plastic uprights. Gently, they reached up and swung the babies down to cradle them in their laps.

'OK?'

'*It feels strange.*'

'*Warm, smooth . . .*'

110

'Hold on tight – I'm going to start the water now.'

She filled an empty yoghurt pot with water from the cold tap and slowly poured it through the wide funnel, so that the falling water began to turn the plastic paddles. The two Waterfolk stared fearfully at the erratic water flow.

'Is this going to be OK? It won't be for long – just a temporary measure.'

'*It is not as good as the waterfall you took us to,*' said one.

'I know, but that was too dangerous,' Jo apologised.

'*This is better than the small place of the tempest,*' the other acknowledged.

It was the first positive response she'd received. Jo, trying not to notice the other creature, trembling nervously as the water sloshed in front of it, confined her thoughts to the first.

'I've got another problem,' she confessed. 'I can't stand here emptying pots of water on to you all day. I'll have to think of something else.'

'Jo!' her mother's voice came up the stairs. 'You all right?'

'Yes, I'm fine. Just coming.'

She flushed the toilet vigorously and the water gushing round the toilet pan set her thinking again. 'I wonder . . . Look, hold on, you two. I'll move you under the tap and leave it on for now.'

She put the whole wheel on the bottom of the bath and turned the tap above them half on, so

111

it released just enough water to keep the paddles turning.

'I'll be back soon,' she promised as she unlocked the door. 'Sweet dreams!'

Outside, sprawled on the grass but with her mind on the Waterfolk, Jo found it hard to concentrate on her mother's conversation.

'I said, "Are you feeling all right?" Cloth ears!'

'Oh – yes, fine.'

'How did you get on? Catch anything?'

'What?' Jo was alert, heart thumping. 'How do you mean?'

'You went fishing, remember? What do you think I meant?' Jo's mum was always quick to latch on to things not being said.

'Oh! Nah, water was too low.'

'Well, what did you do all day, then?' She would keep on and on.

'Nothing,' Jo said.

Her mother gave her a look.

The Blob, by this time grizzly and covered in mud and daisy petals, had got hold of Jim's empty glass. Snatching it away was guaranteed to produce a protest at any time, but at the end of a long hot day he was inconsolable.

'Bath time, definitely,' Jo's mum declared.

'Oh hang on, Mum. I need a . . . the toilet.' Jo jumped up immediately and, ignoring her mother's puzzled stare, ran up and locked herself firmly into the bathroom.

The little creatures were still sitting on the

platform, but slumped now, heads lifted but eyes hooded by a milky blue skin.

'Sorry to interrupt. Quick, hop on!'

Unused to any necessity for speed, the Water-folk hefted the youngers on to their hips and clambered groggily on to the spoon. As soon as Jo immersed them in the jamjar, though, they whisked their tails and twisted and turned with renewed vigour.

The door handle rattled. 'You got an upset stomach, Jo?' her mother called.

'No!' She pulled the flush again and, putting the jar behind her back, slipped out of the bathroom.

Fizz was not a usual visitor to the house. He preferred to wait for people to call him out. Even this time he didn't come to the front door, but rode his bike down the narrow alleyway at the side of the house, knocking into the watering-can with his front wheel and sending it clattering. Propping himself against the wall, he pulled the chewing gum from his mouth with one hand and whistled through the thumb and index finger of the other.

Jo appeared instantly, forgetting even to be surprised. 'Where did you go just when I needed you!' she attacked him.

'What?'

Quickly but dramatically, Jo told him of the potential disaster and her heroism, ending with the latest dilemma: how to find a safe hiding-place for the Waterfolk.

It was Fizz who came up with the garden-hose solution. He'd noticed the hose when he cycled into the watering-can. Before the hose-pipe ban, Jim had used it to water his vegetables.

'Put the hose into the watering-can. Fill the can right up, keep the tap running very slowly and the can'll just keep overflowing.'

As Jo's doubtful look didn't disappear immediately, Fizz leapt off his bike and set about demonstrating how his scheme would work until they were both standing in a wash of cold water.

'Yeah, OK.' Jo was forced to concede it *was* a workable idea and the tap being at the side of the house made the whole thing safer.

'We could build them a little shelter under the water,' she added, gathering up a few stones and constructing a small grotto near the drain cover, where the excess water could drain away.

This time it had to be without the aid of the slotted spoon that she moved the Waterfolk to their new premises. She scooped at the water with her fingers and explained the changed circumstances to them as she did so.

'Just climb on my hand, right into the palm – I'll let the water dribble out between my fingers. Oh, you're tickling!'

'Let me do it.' Fizz was looking over her shoulder jealously.

'It's OK,' said Jo. So far, she had been the only one to handle them. 'You turn the tap on.'

They stood for a moment side by side, mesmerised by the overflowing water.

'That'll do for now, but I've got to think of something else long term,' Jo told Fizz. Suddenly it came to her. 'Got it! Tash, in Wales! She's got a waterfall and everything just near her. I'll take them there!'

'I'll come,' Fizz volunteered but both of them knew he wouldn't be able to. He wouldn't be able to find money for the fare, for a start.

'I'll go Tuesday, after we break up . . . I'll take them on the bus after school. We'll just have to keep them in the school for the morning somehow. Maybe you can think of something,' she said more gently.

Fizz nodded and cracked an air bubble in his gum against his front teeth. He turned and swung his leg over the cross bar of his bike, and, putting his feet up to either side of him, one on the brick wall of the house, the other on the fence, he scooted backwards down the alley and out of sight.

# 12

After Fizz had gone, Jo's thoughts immediately turned to Tash. She could leave an urgent message with . . . what was his name? She found Tash's letter and stuffed it in her pocket, grabbed some silver coins from her purse and sauntered downstairs, trying to appear normal.

'Just popping out to the shop,' she told her mother. 'Got to get a paper for homework.'

'What sort of paper? We've got hundreds here,' said her mother.

'No, it's got to be today's – local. Can I get you anything?' Jo added quickly.

Outside the corner shop there was a phone box. Quickly, Jo dialed the number. It took a long time for anyone to answer.

'Please be there! Please!' Jo was begging.

She checked the number. Llandovery 243 – Weirdo. She couldn't call him that!

'Yeah.' There was someone there.

'Hello. Have you got a dog called Robocop?'

'What if I have? Who is this?'

'And three cats called Terminator?'

'Two – Terminator Three got shot.'

'Oh, sorry.'

'It's OK. Look, who is this?'

'This is Jo. I'm a friend of Tash's. You know, Shaun's her dad.'

'Oh yeah. Tash, yeah.'

'I've got a message for her. It's very urgent, life or death! She's got to phone me – Jo – immediately.'

'What, now? This evening? Can't it wait?'

'No, it can't! Could you possibly . . . please! It's so urgent.'

'Well, OK. Perhaps you can do something for me one day.'

'Anything,' Jo said rashly.

Jo arrived back panting and hovered round the phone anxiously until it rang within the hour.

'Tash?' she said loudly with false surprise, closing the door with her foot and crouching down behind the settee to muffle the sound as far as possible.

'Jo! Got your message. What's going on?'

'I've got to come and stay,' Jo whispered.

'Great! When?'

'Tuesday, after school. It's urgent!'

'Why, what's up?'

'The creatures – the blue things . . . Oh, I'll explain when I see you. I've looked up a coach, 9.30 at Brecon. That's the nearest. Can you get your dad to agree, and come and meet me?'

'I expect so, but what's – '

'I'll explain everything, promise. I'm bringing them with me!'

'What?'

Jo cut her short. 'Don't worry, it'll be fine. Gotta go . . .'

'What's wrong with your voice?'

'Nothing. And Tash? Can't wait!'

'Me neither!'


'How on earth did *that* happen?' Jim appeared in the kitchen doorway. Jo and her mother were watching television and Jim had strolled outside to inspect his vegetables. 'Did you leave the hosepipe on?'

'The hosepipe?' repeated Jo's mother. 'No, of course not. There's a ban on.'

'Exactly! Jo, do you know anything about this? Jo?'

Jo shook her head, gazing intently at the screen and hoping her face did not betray her thumping heart.

'The entire side of the house is awash. Hope the woman next door doesn't report us. She's just the type who would,' Jim said.

'*You're* just the type who would,' Jo's mum pointed out.

The programme finished. Jo sauntered to the fridge and helped herself to a Coke.

'Jo!' her mother said angrily. 'You might have asked!'

'Can I, Mum, please?' She had already pulled the tab and now gulped thirstily. 'Think I'll go outside for a bit and cool down.'

Having wandered nonchalantly out into the garden, Jo dashed round into the side passage.

Sure enough, the watering-can stood empty; the young beans in the vegetable patch had glistening leaves. By the drain, the ground was dark and damp. The little pile of stones was still there but tumbled over. Carefully she picked up each one, hopeful of seeing a shimmer of blue. Nothing!

'Oh no! Where are you?' With increasing panic, Jo searched the area, turning over stones, unstacking flowerpots, separating seed boxes. 'Don't have disappeared – please!'

'*We haven't, not yet. We are so tired. Help us, please.*'

Overjoyed to catch this pale thought, Jo redoubled her efforts. 'Where are you? Give us a clue.'

'*We are hanging – and below it is dark and empty.*'

'Hanging?'

'*By our arms. But we are afraid to climb up into the air.*'

'The drain! Are you in the drain?'

'*We do not know.*'

The metal drain cover, of course! Lucky if they hadn't been washed away. Jo got down on all fours. Sure enough, as she squinted, she thought she could just see two pearly drips on the side of one of the iron bars.

'Look, I've only got my Coke can, there's still some in it. It's wet, anyway.'

'*We do not understand.*'

'OK. Don't worry. Can you climb up? I don't think this thing moves.'

She wrenched the grid, but it didn't move. 'No – you'll have to climb up.'

Fortunately the Waterfolk's bodies were supple. They swung round like little gymnasts and rose into the air, rather like blue snails which had lost their shells. For a terrible moment, she couldn't see the babies.

'Where are the little ones? They haven't fallen off, have they?'

'*No, they are safe, but it is hard for them. They are very weak.*'

This time the Waterfolk had wrapped their tails round each younger, looping them into safety, holding them as they hung above the emptiness. But they needed their tails for swimming. As they released their grip, so they hauled their way like tiny koala bears up the spangled tails to cling again round Axos' and Odol's shoulders.

Jo spat on her finger and then stretched it towards them. They wrapped their limbs tightly round her and as she moved her hand she felt the tension give as they released their hold.

'Quick, into the can.'

She held her finger over the opening where the ring pull had been and shook it gently. She heard the plop as they hit the liquid. Immediately, there followed cries of pain.

'Oh no, it's the Coke! You'll only stay in there for a second. Be patient!'

Realising she didn't have to hear their complaints if she cut her mind off from them, and not wanting to think about what was happening, Jo rushed back into the house, aiming to reach the bathroom before her mother heard her. Unfortunately her timing wasn't good enough. Her mother was just coming out of the kitchen as Jo ran through.

'What's up with you? You are acting strangely today, Jo!'

'Goodnight!'

'Where are you going with that can?'

'Haven't finished yet.'

'If I find any more empty cans upstairs . . .'

'You won't!' Jo called from the bathroom. 'Oh no!' The jamjar had disappeared along with the slotted spoon.

Back in her bedroom, Jo looked round for inspiration. Pencil case? It would leak. No vases, no containers, no empty cups, nothing . . . Then she saw her old and abandoned doll's house. 'That's it! There's a bath and a sink, room for one pair in each!'

She could pour in some water and then they could haul themselves out using the taps. And they'd be safe in the doll's house overnight. She dashed to the bathroom again and poured some water into a mug, returning to her bedroom to fill up the tiny containers in the doll's house.

'OK, OK. I'm putting this pencil into the tin – hold on tight and then I'll transfer you again.'

Bedraggled and forlorn didn't really describe

them. Their limbs were brownish and tarnished, their green eyes reproachful. The babies were so weak they looked like the lifted skin of a graze too light to bleed.

'Quick, put those poor babies into the water! Here, you scrub yourselves down too. It's clean.'

Suspiciously, they tested the water, but when they found it didn't sting their bodies or frizzle round their nostrils, they sank back more happily – one pair in the bath and one in the sink.

Jo waited and watched them just long enough to see the blue glow coming back into their bodies. It was funny seeing them lying where once her pipe-cleaner dolls had taken their baths without the help of water.

'You'll be all right now, won't you? I'll put you side by side, then you can chat. You can pull yourselves out, can't you? I've got to go now. It's *my* time for dreaming.'

It was while Jo was brushing her teeth the next morning, having checked that the Waterfolk were looking good and blue, that she had her brainwave. She always pulled the toilet chain just before she left the bathroom, leaving it to the last moment because of a crazy idea that the loo water could somehow come down the tap where she was rinsing her mouth.

'Of course, perfect! Not the toilet bowl – the cistern.'

Very carefully and quietly, she lifted the lid

off the tank and looked inside. From out of a small double hole near a large brass bolt, water was gushing. But as the ball-cock came to rest on the level, the water stopped.

'If I could just clip on something . . . The soap-rack from the bath – that's it!'

Delighted with the arrangement, she unlocked the door, peeped round to make sure that all was clear, tiptoed into her room to fetch the doll's house bath and sink and then locked herself back in the bathroom. The transfer made as quickly as possible, Jo explained to the Water-folk that from time to time through the day, the water would gush from the holes above their head. In the meantime they could dive off the soap dish and swim to their hearts' content, swinging back up into the soap dish by clinging to the copper rod.

'Soon,' she promised them, 'we are going to find a *real* waterfall. It'll be dark, mind, when I put the lid on. Now, I mean.'

'*We like the dark.*'

'Well, that's all right then.'

Throughout the day, Jo was a frequent visitor to the bathroom. 'You all right?' her mother said suspiciously. She was making up a thermos for a picnic.

Jo hung her head sadly. 'Don't think I'd better come on this picnic, Mum. I think I've picked up a bug of some kind. I'd rather stay home.'

Her mother felt her forehead. 'No tempera-ture.' She gave Jo a penetrating look, trying to search out the truth. 'Maybe we'll all stay and have the picnic in the garden.' And in spite of Jo's insistence that she'd be perfectly all right by herself, they stayed.

The next morning, Monday, getting ready for school, Jo checked the Waterfolk once more. She removed the porcelain lid and there they were, grouped together in one corner of the soap dish.

'I have to go now,' she said. 'I won't be able to visit you until after school. But tomorrow I will be taking you to the new waterfall.'

'*We do not like it here!*' the Waterfolk complained. '*The water feels strange to our skin and we need a freshness in the air.*'

'I'm doing my best – it won't be long now,' Jo said.

Hearing the front doorbell ring, she quickly replaced the lid.

'Jo!' Jim called up the stairs.

'Coming.' One last look under the lid, and then she pulled the chain.

Fizz was standing waiting for her in the hall, his face full of questions.

'Well, this is an unexpected surprise, Fizz. I haven't seen you for ages,' said Jo's mum cheerfully.

Fizz shuffled his feet in embarrassment. 'I'm going to school with Jo,' he muttered.

'They're in the cistern – I'm leaving them there,' Jo hissed at him as they were getting ready to go.

'Can I just use your toilet, please?' Fizz asked

as they were on the point of leaving. Jo looked daggers at him, wanting to get out of the house as soon as possible.

'You got this bug too?' said Jo's mum. 'There's something going on here,' she said to Jim.

Jo was hopping from foot to foot but just as she heard the flush upstairs, she suddenly remembered she hadn't told her mum about the arrangements she had made with Tash.

'Oh, Mum, I forgot to mention it . . . Tash, when she phoned the other night, she invited me to stay.'

'Oh, that'll be fun. When?'

'Tomorrow.'

'Tomorrow?!'

Jo heard the screech and they were off, dashing down the front path.

Jo knew her mother would be angry, and not even persuading Fizz to come home with her was any protection.

'Hi, Fizz, excuse me a moment while I attack my daughter. Why did you rush out on me this morning, madam? You owe me a few explanations!'

'Can I use the toilet, please?' Fizz asked immediately.

'Go ahead. Jo, I want an answer!'

Jo was cornered. She shot the retreating Fizz a betrayed glance. 'I'm going straight up to Tash's place tomorrow after school – it's all arranged.'

'By whom?'

'Us.'

'I'm sorry, that's not good enough.' The Blob was busy emptying his mother's handbag, which usually made her wild, but having got her daughter on the ropes, she tried to ignore him.

'Go at the weekend – Jim will take you.'

'It's OK. I'm going by coach.'

'Not alone, you're not!'

'I've done it before, to Gran's.'

'That was different.'

'Why?'

'Jo, I need to talk to Shaun at the very least.'

'Why?'

'I'm just trying to be a good parent, Jo. Blob, get out of there! I've got to have something private left!' She picked him up roughly, pulling her make-up pouch out of his hands and making him scream.

'See what you've done?' she threw at Jo.

Fizz came back into the kitchen, managing to make a surreptitious thumbs-up sign to Jo as her mum was handing the Blob a beaker of juice to soothe his hurt feelings.

'Look, Jo,' she continued. 'I just can't see the hurry, and this is me putting my foot down, reasonable or not. You will not go unless I speak to Shaun first.'

Jo knew that when the famous foot had come down, she might as well shut up. There was nothing else to be gained at this stage.

Later, Jo again phoned Llandovery 243 from the phone box outside the corner shop.

'Yeah!'

'Hello, it's me again.'

'Which me?'

'The me who's Tash's friend. I'm really sorry to have to ask you, but could you possibly . . .'

He groaned. 'Not Tash again!'

'No, Shaun. I need Shaun to phone me . . .'

'Is this really urgent?'

'Life or death!'

'Yeah, of course – life or death. Could be yours we're talking about if I should ever meet you!' he added, before slamming the phone down.

Shaun did phone at 9.15. Jo's mum was still wearing a tight-lipped expression and as the call proceeded, Jo could do no more than hold her breath and hope that Tash had done her stuff.

'Shaun? . . . Yes, well they've cooked something up. I can't get to the bottom of it, but something's going on, I'm sure of it . . . Oh well, if you're certain . . . Yes, I suppose so. I just wanted to make sure . . . Well, you know what it's like . . . OK then, Shaun – and thanks very much!'

Jo let her breath out slowly. She heard the click of the telephone receiver from the hall and then her mother re-entered the room.

'Well, it seems . . . I mean, Shaun says it's OK by him, so now it's up to me.'

Jo stopped breathing again and felt anxious.

Her mum, savouring the moment, said, 'If your room is tidy and if you've hung all your clothes up and if you've behaved like a model child between now and tomorrow – Shaun'll be meeting the 9.30 coach at Brecon. S'pose you'd better give him a reason for being there!'

# 13

As Jo washed her hands and face ready for bed, she explained to the Waterfolk the arrangements for the next day. She had lifted the lid off the cistern so she could chat more easily.

'I'll have to put you back in the sandwich box and take you to school – another place,' she explained, as she saw their doubtful green eyes staring up at her from their perch on the soap dish. 'And then I'll put you in the cistern at school for the day. A place like this, not so nice, maybe . . .' She had a vision of the ancient iron cisterns with their old-fashioned chain pulls which never flushed properly. 'And then I'll put you in the box again at the end of the day because we're going on a bus . . . Well, we're going a long way to find another waterfall, a proper one.'

At this last point their bodies seemed to light up. *'We are happy!'*

The Wateryoungers, who always seemed to have their eyes closed by that film of skin, and who turned their heads away and trembled whenever Jo approached, at last faced her. First one and then the other turned from the safety of the older Waterurchins' bodies to look into her eyes. As they turned, the skin shuttered down to reveal two huge green eyes, luminous, magical, and they spoke to her for the first time. *'We are happy! We are happy!'*

'Oh!' Jo gulped. How strange at this moment of all moments to feel so alone. Just her and them. 'Oh . . .' She swallowed again. 'They're so lovely! What are their names? Do they have names?' she asked, then realised with some embarrassment that she hadn't even asked the larger Waterfolk the same question.

*'We have names.'* Axos introduced himself first. *'Axos.'*

And each in turn spoke his or her name, closing that wonderful green eye and bowing.

*'Odol.'*

*'Mox.'*

*'Lol.'*

'And I am Jo,' she told them.

*'It is a good name – a name that has the "O" within. I know you will save us!'* Axos spoke with renewed confidence.

'I hope so. Tomorrow I will take you to my friend, Tash, and she lives near a waterfall. Everything's going to be all right!' Jo told them. 'And now it is my dreaming time again. I'll have to put the lid back on so it will be dark again. Be ready for a rush of water,' she warned.

*'Sweet dreaming,'* they called out.

'Jo, sandwiches!' her mother called upstairs. 'You haven't made them yet.'

Quickly she pulled the chain and padded downstairs in her nightshirt. Jo's mum and Jim were watching the news, some item about a war somewhere, with pictures of helicopters and wounded people being carried about on stretchers, men in battle fatigues running bent double . . . stupid! Jo preferred to block her ears and concentrate on her packed lunch.

The next item, however, caught her attention. It was something about the drought, pictures of dried river-beds, parched lawns and dried corn husks which a farmer with a tired face reduced to dust between finger and thumb. A spokesman from the government came on to the screen talking earnestly to his public, looking them straight in the eye.

'There are many practical steps that can be taken to save water. Use your bath water on the vegetable garden; share your bath with a friend!' he smirked. 'Put a brick in your lavatory cistern – it will halve the water you use each time you flush. And only flush when it's really necessary.'

Even while the official was still talking, Jim sprang to his feet. As Jo licked the butter from her knife, he disappeared into the garden and reappeared with a brick.

'What's that for?' she asked, but her sinking heart already knew.

'Brick in the cistern. I've been meaning to do it for days,' he called over his shoulder as he took the stairs.

'No! Wait!' Jo stood at the foot of the stairs,

the knife still in her hand, but she could hear the chink of the porcelain. She raced up the stairs after him and stood panicking in the bathroom doorway.

'What's this doing here . . .' she heard him mutter. He lifted the soap dish out of the cistern and put it back in the bath. Jo gasped. Then he pulled the flush, studying the flow of water. 'That's quite sufficient.'

Jo screamed. 'That was . . .'

Jim swung round. 'What?'

'A waste of water.'

'Well, yes. I just wanted to see – '

'Have you finished? I'm desperate!'

'Oh, sorry.'

Jo slammed the door after him and with trembling fingers, she picked up the soap dish. Nothing!

'Oh no.' She hardly dared move her feet. 'Could be anywhere, I might tread on them! Maybe they dropped down the loo . . .'

In desperation, she lifted the lid from the cistern. There they were, hanging like a couple of trapeze artists to the arm of the ballcock, the Wateryoungers trembling once again and hiding their faces from her.

'*The water is drying up again.*'

'*A big boulder has fallen.*'

'*There is no water to swim.*'

'Oh thank goodness, you're all right.'

'*A great rock fell from the light.*'

'*We have no room for swimming.*'

'Never mind,' Jo told them firmly. 'At least you're safe. Here's your dish back. Now, I'll see you again in the morning,' she added quickly, hearing her mother's voice again.

'Jo! Come and clean up this mess. I'm not your slave!'

As luck would have it, Jim had a cancellation for the next afternoon and he asked his receptionist not to fill it. 'I'll pick you up at the school gates at three, Jo,' he volunteered over breakfast.

'Thanks,' she mumbled into her cereal.

At 8 o'clock prompt, the doorbell rang.

'That'll be your co-conspirator, I suppose,' her mother said. And as Fizz shuffled uneasily into the room, she said brightly, 'Ah, Fizz! Last day, then.'

'I'll take your sandwiches, Jo,' Fizz volunteered over-loudly, winking in an obvious way. Jo scowled at him. 'Where is it?' he hissed at her.

'Here.' She picked up the box which she had just placed carefully on the bottom stair. Quickly, he secreted it in his shirt, as he had done before.

Jo's mum was busy mixing Ready Brek for the Blob and Jim was on duty at the toaster. The nods and winks had not escaped them. 'Oh, I give up,' she muttered to Jim, but loudly enough for Jo to hear and know that she knew. As she opened the fridge to get the milk, there were Jo's sandwiches, neatly wrapped in clingfilm.

'Jo, here's your lunch. I dread to think what Fizz has got down his shirt.'

'Nothing,' Fizz and Jo answered together.

Knowing there was nothing resembling a soap dish in the school toilets – in fact, often nothing resembling soap – Jo had smuggled theirs out of the house in her school bag.

'I'll do it. Give us it!' Fizz was standing outside the boy's toilet.

'No, the *Girls'*,' Jo said adamantly. 'I've got to get them at break.'

'OK then, but I'll still do it,' he said.

'You can't!'

'Watch me! Jo – lookout,' he ordered. Obviously he'd forgotten his resolution at Tom's cottage.

Fizz had that kind of loose-hipped, confident swagger, learnt from his elder brothers and TV idols, which meant that a path opened in front of him. No one was going to get in his way! He pushed open the door to the Girls' toilets and the two girls washing their hands when he entered immediately hurried out, drying their hands on their jeans as they went, silent, eyes down, only bursting into giggles when they reached the safety of the corridor.

Fizz toed the doors of all the cubicles. All empty; no need to maintain the swagger. Quickly he dashed into the furthest toilet and banged the lid shut with his foot. He put the box on the floor while he jumped up and removed the cistern lid, and hooked the soap dish over the rim before carefully levering the top off the box. He knew how to be careful if that was what was needed.

The creatures stared up at him with doleful expressions. He was about to say something but thought better of it. They were so tiny and strange and their lives were in his hands, so to speak, and it left him trembling.

'Here, let's be having you,' he muttered, putting his hand into the water.

They didn't hesitate but clung to his fingers. It felt strange, tickly. Cupping his other hand underneath the hand which held them, in case of accidents, Fizz jumped up on the seat. It all happened above his head. He put his hand as far over the rim of the cistern as he could and then said, 'Go for it!'

He didn't hear any splash but felt a flutter in the palm of his hand and then nothing. Proud of a job well done, he replaced the lid and automatically pulled the chain, though there was no need. He was just rubbing thoughtfully at the palm of his hand when Mr Hodge walked in, followed by an agitated Jo, mouth opening and shutting like a goldfish.

'Ah, *Mr* Boyce,' Mr Hodge said, laying emphasis on the 'Mister'.

Fizz scowled at Jo.

'Getting rid of the evidence, are we? Flushing it away?'

'Sir?'

'I always did have my doubts about your reading abilities. Do you know you are in the Girls' toilets?'

Behind his back, Fizz made a gallant signal to Jo to get moving. She did so, picking up her sandwich box from the floor where Fizz had left it and pouring the water away, innocently wiping her hands on a paper towel before leaving.

'I suppose you are aware of the spate of thefts that we've been having from the Girls' cloakrooms? No? I've had my suspicions, Mr Boyce, I must admit, had my eyes on you for some time. And now, surprise surprise, I follow you into the Girls' toilets and find you flushing the evidence away.'

'No, sir! I wasn't!' protested Fizz hotly. 'I never took nothing!'

Mr Hodge shook his head. 'Then can you explain what you were doing in the Girls' toilets, if not trying to put me off your scent?'

'Sir?'

'Well, no point in searching you, I suppose, got here a minute too late. But I think we should talk further on this matter. I'll be wanting to see you in my office at three today. Oh, and take that ridiculous cap off, boy!'

'Oh, sir!' Fizz began to protest. He had meant to go with Jo to the bus station. 'It's my last day, sir!'

'Perhaps you should have thought of that before. Crying shame, really. You're going downhill fast, just like the rest of your family.'

Jo, waiting at the door which she held open just a toe's width, was the only witness to this scene, and her view wasn't totally clear. She saw Fizz's gesture and then heard Mr Hodge's roar of fury. The next thing she was aware of was her foot being trampled by Fizz as he made his dash for freedom. Mr Hodge was left standing behind him, red in the face and beside himself with rage.

An account of the incident spread like fire all round the school, setting everyone's eyes alight with excitement. Hardly anyone was ever rude to Mr Hodge – they were all too scared of him. Fizz would miss the party they always had on the last day of term, which was a pity, but he'd miss the detention and that was a victory.

As Jim drove Jo from the school gates at three, she looked to left and right, half expecting Fizz to appear, but there was no sign of him. Having bought Jo's ticket and a bar of chocolate, Jim stood and waited with her for the coach doors to open.

She clutched the sandwich box tightly to her tummy.

'What have you got in there?' Jim asked. 'Did I see something sloshing about?'

Fortunately the driver appeared at that moment and opened the door. While Jim was talking to the driver, checking the time that Jo was due to arrive, she pulled herself up the three steps on to the coach and quickly secreted the box under her seat. Jim followed and put her rucksack on the rack over her head.

Jo was anxious for him to be gone. 'It's OK, you go. I'll be fine.'

Jim checked his watch. 'Well, if you're sure . . .'

Before he went he took his wallet out of his jacket pocket and peeled off two five pound notes. 'Here you are, then. Have a good time.' And he bent down to kiss her goodbye.

It wasn't until he'd gone that Jo realised this was the first time he had done such a thing.

The journey was long and hot. Jo sat with the sandwich box on her lap, the lid securely in place. They hadn't even left the town before she caught a complaint.

*'It's warm in here, we do not like it. It is uncomfortable; it is not to our liking.'*

'I'm sorry, there's not much I can do about it.'

She tried calling the hostess. 'Have you any ice?'

'Ice? We haven't even got a fridge, lovey – just a cool box.'

'There's nothing I can do,' Jo thought firmly.

*'Are we nearly there?'*

*'How much further?'*

Jo blanked her mind and watched the parched countryside slipping past: fields of yellow wheat, dusty and dry; brown, thirsty-looking grass. Under trees, horses and cattle stood with heads miserably low. In spite of her agitation, Jo dozed off and woke to a greener, darker scene, the sky burning pink and orange. She jumped awake and checked her watch – quarter to nine.

'You all right?' She tuned her mind to focus on the box.

*'We are tired . . .'*

*'Hot . . .'*

*'Weak . . .'*

'Nearly there,' she chirped cheerfully. The woman across the aisle smiled at her.

# 14

Jo knew Tash would make sure Shaun got to the station in time to meet the coach. They were both standing waiting for her, accompanied by one dog. For a second, it was so exciting seeing Tash again, Jo just wanted to hold her and hug her and know that it really was her. She could see from the look in Tash's eyes that she felt the same.

Instead, she just said, 'All right?' and Tash said, 'All right?' and then it was all right. There they were, together, in the same place. They beamed at each other without knowing what to do next until the dog sprang up and nearly knocked the sandwich box from Jo's grasp.

'This is Jones,' Tash told her. 'Down!' she said in her fiercest voice. It worked for thirty seconds. 'Evans has had six pups, Jo! They are so adorable.' Then, noticing the sandwich box which Jo was holding up out of Jones's reach, she suddenly stopped in her tracks. 'Is that them?' she whispered, her eyes alight with excitement.

'Shh,' Jo mouthed, frowning severely. She didn't want Shaun getting involved. But while

he was unlocking the van door, she nodded furtively to Tash.

'Down, Jones!' Tash said with fresh seriousness and, taking hold of the dog's collar, she
dragged her round to the back of the van – from
where she barked continually from the moment
she was locked in to the moment she was let out
an hour later.

Jo felt the landscape, the winding roads and
steep hills, the rough bumpy track. She held the
box carefully on her lap, feeling the weight of
water moving around and imagining the
Waterurchins, the babies on their backs, moving
as the water moved. She imagined that, but
would not allow herself to hear their protest.
Tash, sitting close by, kept glancing at her.
Sensing her worry, she did not attempt much
conversation, although there was so much to say.

'We can take them up tomorrow,' she
mouthed. 'The river's good and high – lots of
rain.' Jo put a warning finger to her lips and
nodded her head towards Shaun.

Eventually they came to a halt. From the
window she could see a group of caravans,
painted dark shades and set in a compound of
natural fencing. Shaun switched off the head-
lights and Jones stopped barking. All Jo could
see was a succession of shapes and shadows,
dark hills behind them and a lighter sky
overhead.

Elaine came out to greet them with a lamp.
She had a shawl wrapped round her shoulders

and big boots on her feet with the laces undone. 'Hello, Jo! Welcome,' she said in a sleepy voice. 'Forgive us country folk, early to rise and early to bed. Make sure Tash looks after you, and we'll talk properly in the morning. Goodnight!'

'Do you want anything, Jo?' Shaun asked. 'Hungry? Thirsty?'

Jo shook her head quickly. She was hopping from foot to foot in agitation, willing the adults to go so she could take the lid off the box.

'Don't forget to put the dog out, Tash,' Shaun called as he turned to follow Elaine.

Jones, hearing this, flattened her ears and slipped in like a shadow as Tash opened her caravan door and flicked on the light.

'Come on, then. Let's see!'

Jo put down the box, pulled back the lid, and both girls peered into the water. Jo gasped in distress.

'Where are they?' Tash asked. 'I can't see anything.'

Jo didn't answer. She was lifting the box up to examine it against the light. 'There they are,' she said in relief. 'Look, in the corner. I'm sorry it's been such a journey,' she added, addressing the Waterfolk. 'Please don't fade away now. It won't be much longer, I promise you.'

'You didn't tell me they could speak,' Tash accused her, peering over Jo's shoulder into the polythene box. 'I still can't see them.'

'There they are, in the corner.'

'Oh, I've got them now!' Tash squeaked in

delight. 'They're tiny. Oh, look! They've got babies on their backs! They're all blue and they've got little arms. They're just like you said!'

'And they don't speak exactly – well, not like we do,' Jo explained. 'You just have to hear them in your head. It's like tuning in a radio: keep turning the dial until you can hear them.'

Tash looked at her as though she were mad.

'Go on!' Jo said. 'Just try.'

Jo put her fingers into the water and the two little Waterfolk pulled themselves wearily out. Their eyes were reproachful.

'This is my friend, Tash.' Jo spoke to them again. 'She knows a waterfall near here, and we're going to take you there tomorrow.'

*'Take us now.'*

'We can't – it's too dark.'

*'Dark time is good time. It must be now!'*

'We could,' Tash said to Jo. 'There's a full moon and, anyway, I know the way. Let's do it!'

Jo flashed her a smile. 'You see, you can hear them,' she said.

'Clear as clear!' said Tash proudly. 'Did you get that?' she said to the Waterfolk. 'We're going right now. You've just got to last out as long as it takes us to get there.'

The creatures said nothing, just slid back from her fingers, entering the water with barely a ripple. Jones, hiding quietly under the bunk, felt the girls' excitement and sprang out, ears alert and ready for action.

The full moon had risen over the hill tops, lighting the valley with a weird radiance. It was easy to pick out the hazards: fallen logs, bramble thickets, dark piles of sheep dung. Together they raced across the first field, Tash leading the way, Jo holding the sandwich box against her chest. At the far side they squeezed through a gap in the hedge, Jones hot on their heels, but the next field was full of sheep, white luminous shapes glowing eerily against the dark of the grass.

'Oh, no.' Jo stopped in her tracks.

'It's OK. She's obedient. Heel, Jones!' Tash commanded fiercely and immediately Jones slunk along behind her, tail and head down, only her ears and eyes alert and focused on the sheep.

At the far side of the second field was another dark hedge of blackthorn, silhouetted against the night sky. This they managed to squeeze through, hardly registering the scratches on their bare arms and legs. Jo could hear the river long before she could see it. The ground fell away in a steep slope, but young oak trees helped their descent to the river below.

Suddenly, there it was, full and gushing, fluorescent white water under the moon.

'Upstream is better,' Tash shouted above the roar of the water.

And sure enough, after a few minutes of leaping upstream from pale moon boulder to pale moon boulder, they came to a series of small waterfalls.

'This is far enough,' Tash said. 'There are

pine forests further up and they're really dark and creepy. I don't like it up there. This one's the best, I think.' She pointed to the first fall with a drop of just a foot or so. The water channelled through a narrow gap between hard and blackened boulders and poured down with such force, it looked almost solid. Below the fall, the water swirled to the right before being pulled away in another small descent to the left.

'And it won't dry up?' Jo asked anxiously.

'Never. It's always raining here, drains off the mountains. Got lots of water in Wales,' Tash said proudly.

It was with more than a twinge of sadness that Jo peeled back the plastic lid from the box. For one sickening moment she thought she was too late.

'Where are the babies?' she panicked, but as Axos and Odol turned, now nearly as pale as the polythene box that held them, their colour blanched in the moonlight, she saw the fading smudges on their shoulders, as though the water itself had formed solids from all that churning.

'We're here! Your new waterfall, at last,' she told them softly.

*'Quick! We must go now. Release us, please!'*

There wasn't time to say anything more, Jo could see that. Gently she dipped her finger into the water, and this time with only the faintest tickling, she felt them clinging to it.

'I'll put you in the water just above the waterfall. You will have to manage then, find your dream places behind it,' she whispered.

She expected another plea, a further whimper or cry of desperation, but nothing came. Then one of the creatures turned his head towards her. Though in this strange X-ray light she could hardly see his outline, and she could read the lines of her palm through his body, Jo could still feel a substance in her hand.

As he turned, he opened his one pale eye. *'Bring us to mind in your dreamings and we will always be there. Remember the food in dreamings!'*

Tash was standing on a purplish rock just above the largest waterfall and reaching out her hand. 'Come on, catch hold!' Gently she pulled Jo up, careful not to dislodge the Waterfolk.

Jo stood uncertainly, delaying the moment.

'Let me see,' Tash demanded. Jo held her hand up one last time so they could see these two jellied beings, each with a miniature form just visible on their backs, like tiny halos of light.

'Quick! They've almost gone,' Tash said.

Jo bent down while Tash held on to the belt of her shorts as she stretched out as far as she dared. Slowly, she submerged her hand in the cold water. There was a quick wriggling movement in the palm of her hand and they were gone.

The two girls stood for quite some time, staring at the water. They clambered downstream and peered into the waterfall, following the luminous whipped-up surface water into the eddies of the pool below, but saw nothing.

'Are you all right?' Jo called out, but there was no reply.

After Jo had repeated her question for the fifth time Tash took her arm. 'They' ll be fine. Let's go.'

They pulled their way up the mossy bank, whistled for Jones, who had been following her own nose along the river bank downstream, and walked slowly back through the oak trees and across the fields of sheep.

'You did the best you could. I mean, you saved them. They would definitely have died if not for you,' Tash told her.

But Jo was miles away, her thoughts turning and tumbling, floating and falling.

She was moving through water, black as tar, chasing something: a light that flickered on and off like a fire-fly in front of her. She squeezed through the rock, rolled on to her back, and then suddenly she was in a chamber flooded with bright light, hot and yellow. Her legs were chained, she couldn't move, and something was squeaking beyond in the bright light.

Jo woke startled, her heart thumping. Across her legs lay Jones, who knew she shouldn't be there – Jo could see that from the guilty expression in her eyes and the way she kept her head down and wagged her tail. The door to the caravan was open: presumably Jones was responsible for that. Bright shafts of hot morning sunlight were streaming in. It was late, had to be. It was that kind of brightness.

She'd been dreaming. They'd gone, the Waterfolk . . . last night . . . She lay back, her face relaxing. 'Phew!' she muttered and reached a hand out to fondle Jones's ears. Then she heard it again, that squeaking, and this time she was awake. It was coming from underneath Tash. Gently, Jo eased her legs out from under Jones and padded across the linoleum floor to lift the blanket which fell like a screen from Tash's bunk to the floor.

She was aware of a strange vibration and thumping of the floor coming through her bare feet. As she knelt, the squeakings became louder and she found herself enveloped in a sweet mealy smell. Lifting the blanket higher, she revealed Evans and her six pups.

'They're one week, one day old,' came Tash's voice from above her, still thick with sleep.

'Can I hold one?' asked Jo.

'Go ahead. Evans won't mind, will you?' The dog flattened her ears when she heard her name and her tail flicked up and down.

Gently, Jo lifted one up. It was only the size of her hand, its head broad as its body. From each corner, a little leg dangled weakly, and the tiny tail was just an afterthought.

Tash leant over the side of the bed and picked out another of the puppies, which she held to her face and smothered with sleepy kisses.

'This one is Panda – yours is Magic.'

Jo put Magic in her lap. He grunted a couple of times and squirmed forward, awkward as a seal.

'He likes you,' Tash told her. 'Can you have one?'

'Oh yes!'

'Did you ask your mum?'

Jo bit her lip. 'Not exactly. But she couldn't say no, could she?'

Later that day, after a huge fry-up – last night's supper, today's breakfast and lunch combined – they decided to write a brief note to Fizz. He might not receive it but they both agreed that he was part of this and he had a right to know what had happened.

'Wish we could just phone him,' said Jo as she pushed the button on the top of Tash's biro.

'Wish he could phone us and tell us he's all right,' said Tash.

'I know, we could write to him with the number of the phone box here and tell him a time to phone!'

Tash was looking doubtful. 'We'd better give him plenty of time. Tell him next Friday, your last night.'

And so they did.

Dear Fizz
Mission accomplished. Safe behind the

waterfall again. We did it! Are you on the run?

Phone us at _____ on Friday and tell us.

Love, Tash and Jo

Before they sealed the letter, they wandered down to the nearest phone box to copy the number on to it. The box was an old-fashioned one with thick red paint that looked like papier mâché. The door was so heavy both girls had to heave it open.

'Pooh! Smells like the Gents!' Jo said, clapping her hand over her nose.

'How do you know?'

Both girls giggled.

'Anyway – probably is the Gents!' Tash added cheerfully.

Jo pinched her nose between her fingers and spoke like a Dalek. 'I'll read the number, you write it down.'

'I put the code too,' Tash said, licking the envelope.'Now at least we've tried.'

Though the girls returned every day to the waterfall, they never did receive any proof positive that their mission had been successful, but somehow Jo became more and more convinced that the Waterfolk were safe, tucked away behind the fall of water.

'Glad *you* saw them too. Anyone would think I was nuts if I told them.' Jo and Tash were sitting watching the puppies playing. The scratches on their arms and legs had almost vanished over the ten days Jo had been staying, and the puppies had changed from barrel-shaped bodies with four little paddles, one at each corner, to upright wobbly creatures with ears that pricked up and legs that sometimes bore their weight.

Magic was Jo's; this was definite so far as she was concerned. The only stumbling block was going to be persuading her mother. There would be a battle, but it was one she felt certain of winning. Somehow, she knew she could count on Jim.

In the first telephone call, Jo had merely told her mother about all the puppies, how adorable they were, and assured her mother that, were she to see them, she would find them utterly irresistible. Her mother didn't seem quite so certain. Jo mentioned Magic specifically on the two subsequent calls, but her mother didn't seem that interested, nor did she understand what Jo was angling for.

On the fourth call, near the end of Jo's stay, Tash and Jo were squashed into the telephone box in the lane as usual.

'Jo? I've got some good news . . .' her mum began.

'What?' Jo's hopes soared for a moment, thinking there might be news of either the puppy or Fizz, and then sank.

'Jim's brother has a cottage in Devon. We're all going at the weekend. It'll be lovely, Jo – a

proper beach holiday. All together, with Gran.
We've missed you, you know, all of us!'

'But what about Magic?'

'Who?'

'Magic! My puppy.'

'No pets, Jim's brother said so. And what do
you mean, "my puppy"?'

'I don't mean take him on the holiday, he's
too little to leave his mum yet. I mean later . . .
Can I keep him, Mum?'

'Well, you know what I think about dogs in
cities, Jo. It's just not fair.'

'Please, Mum! I'll come on the holiday, I'll be
an angel for ever. I'll love the Blob and be nice
to Jim. Please!'

'And I take it you'll hate me if I say no?'

'Yes.'

'Well, I suppose so, then . . . but you've got to
look after him, Jo. He's your responsibility.'

From the outside, two girls could be seen
jumping silently up and down in the phone box,
but when they opened the door and spilled out
on to the road, their whooping and shouts of joy
filled the quiet valley.

Even the sadness of Jo's departure and their
separation was lifted by the thought that the two
girls would be seeing each other soon, when Jo
came to collect Magic. It was another link that
would be forged between them for ever.

On the final Friday evening, at dusk, with the
blackbird pouring out his optimistic song from

the top of the telegraph pole, Tash and Jo went down to the phone box. This was when Fizz was due to ring, though they didn't hold out much hope. They sat side by side outside on the scruffy grass. Tash was tossing little pieces of gravel scuffed up by cars back on to the tarmac where they belonged. Jo had picked herself a long flat grass stem and was making a whistle.

Suddenly the phone started to ring. The girls looked at each other, frozen, for half a second, before leaping to their feet and pulling the heavy door open.

In fact, it was Jo who got to the receiver just before Tash. 'Fizz?' she said, before she'd even heard his voice.

'Jo?' It was Fizz. She nodded to Tash. 'Where are you? What happened?'

To her annoyance, Tash grabbed the receiver. 'Fizz?' she said. 'No, it's Tash! Tash. It was Jo. What happened? Yeah, I heard!'

In a frenzy of impatience, Jo wrestled the receiver from her again just in time to hear him explaining that the money was running out and yelling his number over the beeps. Jo screamed the number out to Tash, but of course, they had nothing to write with. They just had to remember. Before Fizz's voice had left her ears, Jo was punching the numbers. At least they had thought to bring some coins with them.

She heard a distant ringing at the other end, she knew not where.

'Tash?'

'No, it's Jo. Just tell me! What's been going on?'

'Came round, didn't he. Hodge! Asked me to go round to his place cos he had a hedge needed cutting and some gardening jobs and that. So I went round. And I did them.'

'Is that all?' asked Jo, almost disappointed.

'What?' asked Tash.

'I just mowed the grass and clipped the hedge and then I had a cuppa and went home.'

'A cup of tea!' It was beyond belief.

'What?' Tash asked again.

'He lives with his old mum and she's in a wheelchair and she's all shaky and he has to feed her. She was all right, though. Good cake!'

This time Jo passed the receiver to Tash. Fizz must have given her the shorter version because she was soon telling him about the expedition to return the Waterfolk.

'We haven't actually spotted them,' she was telling him. 'They must be all right, though. Why wouldn't they be?'

Jo had fed the last ten pence into the slot before passing the receiver to Tash. As the digits started flashing their warning, Tash only had time to gabble the story of the puppies when a long single beep cut across their conversation. She yelled goodbye, knowing he couldn't hear her. With a shrug, she put back the receiver and both girls started the climb back up the hill to the caravan. They didn't say much. It was finished somehow.

*Behind the waterfall, they have made their home, Axos and Odol. They have fashioned dream spaces: two larger ones to fit their growing bodies, two smaller ones for Mox and Lol. Here they may dream their dreams – dancing dreams, singing dreams, swimming dreams – while their shimmering limbs relax deeply. Behind this curtain of water they are safe again. Through it, the light filters its beams of blue and mauve.*

*Axos and Odol have fashioned combs from fragments of slate and they sit, Mox and Lol in their laps, and groom first the shorter hair of the younger folk, then each other's. Their tangles have long gone and their tresses are growing longer, sleeker. The cold of winter invigorates them, makes their dreams sparkle, and the sharp light of winter lifts their spirits and makes their scales shine like diamonds.*

*Sometimes they throw thoughts to and fro: ideas, hopes, and sometimes even memories of their terrible ordeal, the nightmare, the black time before this place. On the floor of the new grooming chamber, they have collected and set out a small circle of river pebbles. It is Odol who arranges them, sometimes washing them carefully in water scooped from the river. They do not know exactly why they do these things, but it seems right to do them.*

*As they groom, Axos tells tales: old stories, the ones they love, that connect them by an invisible thread to the grooming circles which were before. And he tells the tale of the Paddlefeet, too, to keep them ever-present, to remind them how the Waterfolk* were brought from the edge of nothingness to the fullness of new life.

On most mornings now, when their eyes open to the pale light of a new dawn, all four Waterfolk slip sideways through the water curtain into an illuminated world, to explore the deeper waters, swirling and twirling in the eddies and flurries.

Occasionally Axos and Odol share a thought about the fish. Strange, to them, to have so much water and so few fish to swim with. They remember how they played before with the fishes and tadpoles and all the other water creatures. Sometimes, too, they share a thought about the weeds where they used to tumble and play, twining their limbs round the flailing tentacles for camouflage. In this place, there are none. And sometimes they talk about the strange dead quality of the water against their bodies and they notice the dullness of their scales.

From time to time they share these thoughts, but not often, and not when Mox or Lol might catch them, for they do not wish to cast shadows over their new happiness. Mostly, they are content to live in the ease of the new order, accepting that things are different here: not so colourful, with fewer visitors and less abundance of life. A quieter existence brings with it fewer worries, less chance for further mishap – or so they hope. After all, they are at the beginning of another cycle, another chapter still to be written. They came so close to being part of an end.